EXPIRED PLOT

LAST CHANCE COUNTY - BOOK 6

LISA PHILLIPS

TWO DOGS PUBLISHING, LLC.

Copyright 2020 Lisa Phillips

All rights reserved. This book or any portion thereof may not be reproduced or used in any manner whatsoever without the express written permission of the publisher except for the use of brief quotations in a book review.

eBook ISBN: 979-8-88552-050-8

Paperback ISBN: 979-8-88552-051-5

Publisher: Two Dogs Publishing, LLC. Idaho, USA.

Cover design: Ryan Schwarz

Edited by: Jen Weiber

1

There wasn't much to pack for her interview, and she refused to contemplate the fact her entire life amounted to not even enough to fill one suitcase. If she got this job, Hollis wasn't coming back to Last Chance.

Not ever.

She looked around the quiet of her apartment to make sure she hadn't forgotten anything. She had the rest of her clothes, not counting the black pant suit and white shirt she was wearing, and she'd safely stashed the emergency wad of cash she'd been amassing the past few months. A few toiletries. Enough to get her started somewhere else.

The closet. Hollis pulled her leather jacket from the hall closet and stowed the final item in the suitcase. That brown leather jacket was the only thing she'd ever splurged on in her life. It had been on sale at two hundred fifty dollars. It would really be quite fitting if she wore it while leaving the only town she'd ever lived in. The place she'd spent every day of her life.

No. It didn't matter what she wore. It only mattered that she was finally free of it all. No more trying to do the right thing. No more trying to get everyone to see what was right in front of their faces. She was done. Her life was going to be lived on her own terms from now on.

Hollis grabbed the letter she'd written to the man who owned the lease on the diner she'd run ever since her stepfather, Frankie, had been in an accident. She would leave the letter in the office after she said her final goodbyes to the place she'd spent nearly half her life and the only job she'd ever had.

A lump rose in her throat.

"No." Her voice sounded thick, but still hollow. She wasn't going to cry.

She pulled out her phone and sent a text to the guy she'd been seeing for the past couple of weeks now.

I won't be able to make dinner tomorrow. Sorry.

They were supposed to have been going to some concert for date number six. She didn't feel super bad about leaving him—or so she was trying to convince herself. After all, she was pretty sure there was something he was keeping from her. It was mildly irritating that she would never find out what it was. But not irritating enough to stop her from doing what she had to do.

She breathed a big sigh of relief. She was finally leaving Last Chance, going somewhere none of them would ever be able to find her. Where the past wasn't going to hold her back, or hold her down.

"No more."

It was like an addiction. She had to cut them all off cold turkey, or she'd never get free of it. She would never find something genuine that was just hers. People with no ulterior motives. Hollis was going to get a fresh start where no one knew her.

Her phone buzzed. The repeated buzzing told her it wasn't a text. She turned it to look at the screen and saw *Dad* illuminated. He was actually her stepfather, but given how flaky her mother was, it wasn't a surprise that Hollis had gravitated to the only supportive parent she'd ever had. Frankie's first love would always be the diner, which was why Hollis had worked there since the day she turned fourteen. All she'd wanted was to be absorbed into his world.

She swiped to answer. "I've been trying to reach you all day. Where are you?"

"Holl—" His voice cracked.

"Frankie?" She'd never actually called him dad. Not after the first time, and the way her mother had laughed at her for twenty minutes. "What's wrong?"

There was a shuffle on the other end of the line. After that, a voice came on. "We have your father." It sounded like a recording, like in one of those kidnapper movies.

The voice sent a shudder through her, and she swallowed. "What?"

"I won't repeat myself."

Only this wasn't a movie.

"Who are you?" She'd stood up to plenty of bullies in her life. She straightened her shoulders and didn't betray one ounce of fear in her tone. "What do you want?"

The voice let out a low chuckle, detached and emotionless. "They told me you could be cold. Now I believe them. We have your father."

"Where is he? Don't hurt him." She gasped out a breath. "What have you done with him?"

"Enough questions." The voice said, "He stays with us, and we'll send instructions. If you don't do as we ask, he dies. If you involve the police, he dies. If you fail to respond..." The voice didn't finish.

"I get it." Hollis squeezed the phone so hard her hand started to cramp. "I need to speak to—"

"Don't waste my time."

"No—"

The line went dead.

"Frankie!"

Hollis lowered the phone and stared at the screen.

Kidnapped. This was insane. What was she supposed to do,

sit around and wait for instructions? She was supposed to be at an interview! And yet, suddenly, the interview and her plan to leave seemed so pointless.

Trying to leave town.

Starting a new life.

He dies.

Her hand shook, and she had to fight for a steady breath. *We have your father.* He'd been kidnapped. *Father.* That was the word he'd used. Interesting, considering it said he only knew what he'd been told about Hollis. This wasn't someone she considered a friend—who'd know Frankie was no relation of hers.

She looked at the packed suitcase and her purse. She'd been about to walk out the door, leave town, and never come back. Now she was going to have to do…what?

Hollis glanced around her apartment. What could these people even want? And worse, what would they ask her to do to get him back? She didn't even want to imagine. It had to be serious, otherwise why go to the trouble of kidnapping a man and holding him hostage?

She shifted her phone in her grasp and tried to steady the shake in her hands.

She could call the police. Conroy, the Last Chance police chief, was a long-time acquaintance. His fiancé was always nice when she came into the diner to order their lunch. The police detective, Savannah Wilcox, was someone Hollis liked. She could probably consider them all friends. But Hollis didn't have friends. It was just easier that way.

Less of a chance her mother could make a mess of everything, the way she'd been doing for Hollis's entire life.

She winced. Her mother.

Hollis slipped her cell phone into her purse, grabbed her suitcase, and locked her apartment. She slipped the door key into an envelope and put it in her purse so she could mail it after she accepted the new job. The suitcase went into the trunk of her little compact SUV, the car Frankie had handed down to her for a year of low payments when he'd upgraded his own ride.

She drove over to her mother's townhome where Sharleen lived in by herself—that is, when she chose to be alone. The other times, when she didn't want to be by herself, she invited over whoever she wanted. But not Hollis. Sharleen had kicked Hollis out the day she'd turned eighteen, walking away from the lease on their tiny rental house to buy a classy townhome.

Hollis had slept in the diner on the cramped office couch for a month until she found a place of her own.

Before she walked up to the front door, Hollis switched out the suit jacket for her leather one. The brown jacket would hopefully distract her mom from making any sort of conclusion that Hollis had been headed to an interview—or maybe a funeral. Her mom likely wouldn't care either way, but Hollis didn't want to field any questions right now.

And it was none of Sharleen's business.

Her mom answered the door. She took one look at Hollis's jacket. Jealousy flashed in her eyes, but she didn't comment. Then she flipped her hair back and said, "What?" while bracelets slid down her slender, bare forearm.

Hollis lifted her chin. "I need to talk to you."

Sharleen said nothing, even though she had to know something was wrong. She also didn't move. Just stood there in a blouse that probably cost more than what Hollis made in two days, and a pair of jeans Hollis wouldn't be able to fit into even if she went on a starvation diet for two years. Which she knew all too well about—because her mom had actually put her on one. That is, until Hollis had figured out that fast food places had dollar menus. From then on, she'd supplemented her food intake with money she found on the sidewalk on her way to school.

"I need to come in."

Her mom opened the door, but only wide enough for her to

get her own body through. Hollis had to turn sideways. Her mom still didn't budge, so Hollis had to squeeze her way in.

This was a mistake.

Hollis walked all the way to the open living and kitchen area. Then she turned around.

"Frankie's been kidnapped." She took a breath and tried to figure out how to continue. "I'm not supposed to involve the police, but I need help. Why would someone kidnap him?"

"How should I know?" Her mother strode to pour herself a drink at the breakfast bar and slung it back in one gulp. "Why should I care?"

"Maybe you didn't hear me, but he was *kidnapped*. I have to do whatever they want, or they'll kill him."

"Like I said. I'm supposed to care?"

Hollis wanted to scream at her. "There's no one else I can go to. Surely you know…someone who might know who took him. Or why. Or maybe they know who did. You have contacts in town, right?"

Her mom was the only person in Last Chance who might be able to help her and not put Frankie in danger.

Sharleen only chuckled. "I am connected. Maybe I can make some calls."

"I would appreciate it." Hollis gritted her teeth.

"You can do whatever with the information."

"Thank you."

"Don't thank me yet." Her mom slung back another drink. "I haven't done anything."

Hollis stood between the leather couch and the entryway table and waited.

Her mom just stared at her. "What?"

"You're going to make some calls."

"With you here?" She tipped her head back and laughed.

Hollis strode around the breakfast bar and got in her mom's face. This was exactly why she had to leave.

"I know Frankie isn't your favorite person. You both have

your own things going on." It had been years since they were together. "But you must still feel *some* kind of affection for him. Or are you as cold and heartless as you tell everyone I am?"

"Of course, I think fondly of the good times," her mom said. "We aren't all like you."

Hollis didn't have time to even touch that. "So, make your calls, because I'm getting him back."

"You?"

"At least one of us cares."

"Because you've gotten all emotional, suddenly that means you care?" Sharleen poured another glass. "It just means you can't handle yourself."

She lifted the glass to her lips.

Something snapped within Hollis, and she swung out with her arm and hit the glass out of her mom's hand. It hit the sink across the kitchen and shattered into tiny, glinting pieces.

Her mom actually flinched.

Hollis said, "As soon as I get him back, I'm leaving town."

"I know, dear." There was no affection in the word, though it was technically an endearment. Sharleen was the sun, orbited by every planet in the solar system. Shining its light. Shame this sun had no warmth to it whatsoever.

Hollis didn't need to get on a tangent about how her mom could've possibly known that. "Find out who has Frankie."

Hollis had no idea who was holding Frankie, or what they wanted. Maybe her mom could help, or maybe she'd make everything so much worse that Hollis would regret involving her. The way she always regretted involving her mother in anything…for as long as she could remember.

Frankie was the closest thing she had to family. It wasn't like she would leave without getting him back. She'd never be able to live with herself.

Didn't matter that her family was fractured. If you could even call it a family. Her stepdad cared about the diner. Everything—and every*one*—else was a distant second. She'd planned to tell him goodbye, but doubted he'd have stopped her from going to her interview. Or that he'd have done or said more than give her a hug and wish her well.

"Why do you even care, if you're leaving anyway?"

She turned back and saw something in her mom's expression that she couldn't decipher. Not surprising. Sharleen gave nothing away. But that only made Hollis all the more curious. "Because it's Frankie."

Her mom shrugged like she was confused.

"He can hire another general manager." She shrugged. "But he needs to know why I'm not showing up for work on Monday."

She didn't want to leave him in the lurch. And on the off-chance he'd be worried, or even compelled to file a missing person's report, she'd rather have communicated clearly to him.

Not that she expected anyone to come looking for her.

But then, that was the whole idea.

She said, "Just tell me if you come up with something. Because he can't help himself at all right now. He's been *kidnapped*, Sharleen."

Her mom rolled her eyes. "Yeah, I *know*. I said I would make calls, and I will."

Hollis closed the front door behind her. She strode to her car, looking at her mom's street. It was the other end of town from where she lived. Between the two houses were her stomping grounds—all the places she'd walked her whole life. History.

Don't get nostalgic.

The grass wasn't greener anywhere else, but that wasn't what she wanted, anyway. She was only looking for different grass where no one knew her. A place she could make a fresh start with genuine relationships.

Her phone buzzed. She climbed into the front seat of her car and pulled out her phone. An image sent by text. A private number.

Frankie had been roughed up. His hair was matted down on one side, and he had a swollen black eye. He'd been gagged by a roll of cloth.

A whimper escaped her lips. She sent a reply text.

DON'T HURT HIM.

She could imagine the voice on the other end of the phone laughing. Could remember the amusement in his tone. A tear rolled down her cheek. Why take Frankie? What could they possibly want and why hurt him? She could only assume they needed her to do something.

It had to be bad if they thought they needed that much leverage. And it had to be something *she* could do—an asset, or a scapegoat.

Hollis swiped away the tear, and then sent another message.

JUST TELL ME WHAT YOU WANT ME TO DO.

2

Will shut the door to the interview room in the Last Chance Police Department and tossed the file on the table. "I'm FBI Special Agent Will Briar."

The man across the table lifted his brows. "Yeah, I remember you." Stuart Leland had lived in Last Chance for a few months. This was a good guy. A solid guy who was now married to the police department receptionist, Kaylee.

"Yeah?"

"We were in Utah, when Kaylee was kidnapped." Stuart studied him. "Tate said he was bringing the FBI."

"Ah." Yeah, he'd been in on that operation. Taking down a facility owned and operated in secret by a man who talked his way up to the CIA Director job. The FBI had arrested him, lost him and then Last Chance cops had helped them get him back in custody. Will had a hand in that, but it was mostly their doing bringing down Pierce Cartwright.

"Thanks for your help, by the way."

Will nodded. Kaylee had been the focus of Pierce Cartwright's attention, but she was safe now.

And despite Jess Ridgeman and Ted Cartwright's recent

attempts to bring in the local bad guy "West," he wasn't so sure they'd actually accomplished it.

"And this is about…"

Will pulled out the chair and sat. "This isn't a formal conversation, and you're not in trouble."

"But you are fishing for information." Stuart's eyes narrowed. "About what?"

Will saw movement out the door, in the hallway. Conroy—the police chief—stood there, watching. Beside him was Kaylee, this man's wife and the receptionist. She might be happy, married to Stuart, but she wasn't happy right now.

He was out of options. Will had been living in Last Chance for nearly a year now, using the persona of a biker and going by the name "Hammer." A guy who had a spider web tattoo on the side of his neck.

"You work at Hollis's diner, correct?"

Stuart shrugged. "Everyone knows I cook there."

Will could've opened the file, but he knew what was in there. He'd written it. "A week ago on Tuesday, Hollis left the diner around four pm."

"I doubt it," Stuart said. "Considering she never leaves before six."

"And that specific day?"

"Can't say I remember specifics on a random Tuesday."

"Only last week. So, try." Will had a lot riding on this. He needed Stuart to give him something he could go on, because they'd all been trying to bring down West for months. Had they cut off the head of the snake? Will didn't think so.

He'd even tried getting close to Hollis to see if she would let him into her life. All the way in. Because too many things had pointed in her direction.

She hadn't opened up, though.

"Tuesday was the day a couple of kids spilled soda in their macaroni," Stuart said. "I remember because I ran out, so I told them they'd have to wait while I remade it. The mom didn't want to. She got mad. I talked to her, but Hollis wound up giving them something else for no charge. The lady still stomped out."

Will nodded. He'd seen Hollis handle irate customers before and respected the way she was with people. She gave modestly. Neither was she a pushover. Some people would simply never be satisfied.

Will said, "What time did she leave that day?"

"After she closed out the cash register and doled out the tips it was after five."

That was the same time Will had in his notes from the surveillance he'd been doing. "She's the one who handles all the money?"

Stuart nodded. "Though, if I asked, she would let me look at the books. She said that to me the day she hired me. Straight up, if I wanted to make sure I was being paid fairly, I could just ask."

"And she logs all the tips?"

"Notes it all down. Her records are meticulous." Stuart frowned.

Will wasn't going to explain why he was asking about Hollis and the diner money. Her being meticulous could be both a good and bad thing as far as Will was concerned. Either she insisted on everything being above board, or she was particular because she was hiding something and needed to make sure the deception was all straight. So, which was it?

"That's what you want?" Stuart leaned back in the chair. "Information on whether Hollis is dirty, like she's hiding something from everyone? The FBI has better things to do than investigate a waitress in Last Chance. Surely." He shot Will a look.

One he had little trouble deciphering.

Stuart thought Will was an agent no one cared enough about to give significant assignments to, and so he'd been relegated to this.

It was on the tip of Will's tongue to tell this Last Chance resident his current theory about West's real identity. Considering he had no evidence it would only sound outlandish. What he needed was to get the FBI colleague who operated as his handler—FBI Special Agent Eric Cullings, a guy with plenty of local contacts—to send him the tax records for Hollis's diner. Then he might have more than a theory.

He might know for sure who "West" was. The criminal behind every bad guy activity in Last Chance was a person who remained elusive the past few months while Will had investigated drug smuggling. Then the founders emerged, and the cops had been taking them down, one by one. Going up the ladder while the police searched for West as well. A series of cases had led them through the founders of Last Chance—all the way to the boss. The head of the snake had been outed as the fire chief, responsible for most of the crime in town.

Only problem was, the cops were convinced he was "West."

Will was not.

Someone else pulled the strings, and the fire chief was simply the last in a line of scapegoats.

Hollis was a business owner. The diner had been in her family for years, right? He had reason to believe she was "West." Alternatively, if she wasn't, and he was wrong, then Will was almost positive she knew who West really was.

At one point, he'd believed "West" to be a group of people even. Now there was an unpopular theory. But it had weight nonetheless. West, a collective persona. He had that possibility on the back burner, and he would continue to until he figured out exactly what Hollis was hiding.

Will had an idea. "You said she would show you the books if you asked. How about you make me a copy."

Stuart snorted. "Wow."

"Something funny?" If he could get the financial records, then maybe he could prove she was receiving money she should never have access to. Washing it for the criminals in town so they could have it back as legit bills.

"You want me to copy it all to a flash drive while she's not looking?"

"I'm sure you can find the motivation to cooperate."

"All her records are on paper." Stuart shook his head and got up. He strode to the door. "Good luck with your fishing expedition. Though, I'm not thinking your odds are great for catching anything."

He left Will alone in the interview room until Conroy walked in. "You wanna tell me what that was?"

Will glanced over at the police chief. Conroy had worn suits every day as the department's lieutenant. Will would bet he probably wore a suit on the weekend nowadays, too. Now his fiancé held that rank, and he'd been promoted to chief. No one knew when the two would be married. So far in town Tate and Savannah had eloped, and Stuart and Kaylee had been married in a tiny ceremony a few weeks ago. Dean and Ellie were seriously dating, and his brother was seeing her sister.

As far as Will could tell, they were all good cops. Effective and upright. There hadn't been any red flags. Not that he'd seen so far, at least. For a police department anywhere, that was basically unheard of. Which meant, either they hid their wrongdoing well, or they were the most moral bunch of cops he'd ever met in his life.

Will swiped the file off the table as he stood. "Just a couple of questions. Getting a feel for the situation over at the diner."

"Because you think Hollis is West."

It wasn't a question, so Will didn't take it as one. "That's part of an ongoing investigation."

"What Ted and Jess heard was…" Conroy shook his head. "It had to have been a red herring. There's no way Hollis is involved."

"Until you can prove that," Will said, "I have to continue as though it's at least a possibility."

Conroy worked his mouth side to side. No way to argue with that. "Just...tread lightly with her."

"You want me to go easy when she could be West?" Would this be evidence that Conroy wasn't as upright as he'd always thought?

"Of course not." Conroy said, "It's just....you don't know her."

"And you do?"

"I know enough, so I'm telling you this." Conroy folded his arms. "You'd better be sure. Because if you're not and you move on it anyway, I don't want you back in my town. Ever."

"Fine." Will headed for the door while Conroy muttered behind him.

"I know you're trying to date her, too. As Phil Tilley."

Will turned. "So?" He'd made several plays. Hung a few lines out there, both as his undercover biker persona and as the buttoned-up, straight-laced guy Phil. Either the biker discovered evidence his way, or Hollis would give something up. The two personas moved in such differing circles, it wasn't hard to keep someone from recognizing him. So far, at least.

Too many people knew who he really was. Sooner or later he would be outed.

"I get that you wanna finish this undercover assignment. To know you got the guy at the top," Conroy said. "I just don't like how you're going about it."

Didn't matter. Will was going to do this, and how the locals felt about him wasn't his problem. He was beyond tired and wanted to finish it. The need to close the case and walk away was a desperation that wouldn't let him get a full night of sleep. He'd never left anything unfinished.

And this wasn't done.

If he felt any peace at all these days, it was when he saw Hollis's name light up on his phone screen. Whatever that was even about.

Of course, it was Phil Tilley she was calling. Not him. Will had no reason to reciprocate her phone calls at this point. Not when she didn't even know who he really was. Once she found out, he could kiss all their rapport goodbye.

She would know exactly how much he'd been stringing her along this whole time.

That was why he had to push aside his feelings and get this case closed. Get the evidence he needed, and contact his handler for an arrest warrant. Eric would take care of all the paperwork. All Will had to do was make sure there would be no doubt as to the identity of this "West" person they'd been chasing for months.

After that, he could walk away clean.

Done.

Will's phone rang as he walked out. He expected it to be Hollis, following up with her text—as if she'd know he had just been thinking about her—but it was Eric. He sent his FBI agent handler to voicemail and slid the phone into his cup holder before driving to the diner.

From across the street, he watched the front windows.

Hollis opened seven days a week for breakfast and lunch. He knew she ran the place essentially singlehandedly since her father's accident. He'd broken both his legs, which put him in a wheelchair, or occasionally on crutches, depending on how his day was going, but no one knew how it had happened.

Will also knew West was a woman, with a witness description that matched Hollis, and intel that suggested she used her diner to launder money. He was going to prove she'd been behind everything sinister going on in Last Chance this whole time.

The fact he was attracted to her was simply further proof of how convincing she was. Manipulating everyone, all the time. Whenever she wasn't alone, the woman was spinning a line. Creating a story that had the town convinced of how nice she was.

Not him.

He'd seen through her, as much as he'd rather believe it wasn't true. As though she were some kind of innocent bystander caught in the middle.

He didn't believe in that. No one was innocent. Will was even beginning to wonder if the police department here wasn't covering up for her. Perhaps she'd paid them off. Given how Conroy talked about Hollis, it could be that he benefited from some kind of arrangement between the two of them.

That made enough sense that Will decided he'd have to include this new theory in an email to Eric tonight.

Will got out of his car and took a walk around the building, just in case something was happening.

He wandered nonchalantly until he saw the back door was ajar, then pulled his gun and headed inside, still dressed as Will. Jeans, boots, and a dark green Henley. Hard to explain the style change to someone who only knew straight-laced Phil, but he would if he had to. At least he wouldn't have to explain why the biker known as Hammer had no tattoo right now. Will had covered it with makeup, but hadn't bothered to wipe it off when he changed clothes.

By the time it did fade, he planned to have this case all wrapped up. He'd be far from Last Chance and the people here who knew him only as a biker.

Will crept down the dark hall. A light was on in the office, and he could hear someone rooting around in there.

Two steps toward the door, he heard a shuffle. The blow came out of nowhere.

Pain reverberated through Will's skull.

His body slammed onto the floor and everything went black.

3

Hollis froze three steps from her apartment front door. *Home again.* A manila envelope lay propped on the mat against the door. She stared at it like it was going to explode or something.

Part of her wanted to go inside and grab her suitcase, throw it in her car, and take off to her interview anyway. She'd have to completely ignore the envelope. Just leave, never to be seen or heard from again. That sounded glorious…except for the fact she would be wracked with guilt for the rest of her life never knowing what happened to Frankie. Always wondering how it would've turned out differently if she'd actually done something to save him.

Maybe her mom was right and she was cold.

Why else would she contemplate not doing whatever it took to help her stepfather? To keep him from danger? They weren't affectionate. He treated her like he treated everyone else, except that she managed the diner for him and was paid slightly more than the others.

Would he thank her for saving him? Probably.

Would their relationship change at all? Unlikely. Hollis

would still leave. He would probably be more irritated than sad that he had to replace her.

Was it still the right thing that she should at least try to save him? Of course.

She dumped her purse and keys by the doorstep, then picked up the manila envelope. It had no writing on it, and it wasn't addressed to her. Someone had left it for her, though. After they'd told her to wait for further instructions.

Hollis slid her finger in the side of the flap and tugged. It was taped. She grabbed her keys and cut it open using the door key she planned on returning before she left.

That was when she got the feeling she wasn't alone. An instinct of self-preservation told her there was someone out here with her.

Hollis whirled around and saw Conroy walking toward her. The envelope shifted. Something from inside fell out. The chief of police bent and picked up the object, holding it out for her.

"You dropped this."

Hollis snatched it from his hand. She was pretty sure she also scratched him with a nail, but he didn't react. It was a flash drive, black with a red slider—so the part you plug into the port could slide in and out. She stuffed it back into the envelope, sliding her thumb against the edge of a piece of paper that had fallen part way out.

A note.

What was written on it?

"Is everything okay, Hollis?"

She looked up, blinking at him. *If you involve the police, he dies.* Her brain blanked. She didn't know what to say or even what to think. Conroy could help. She didn't doubt that. What she doubted was the kidnapper's ability to keep their word and not simply kill Frankie before she could take action that got him back.

"Hollis."

"Hey." She blinked again. "What?"

"Is everything all right?"

"Sure." She pasted on a smile. Thankfully it came easy, considering she'd been pretending everything was all right for years while her mom did whatever she wanted. With *who*ever she wanted.

Hollis clutched the envelope against her front. Conroy eyed it, then her face, like he knew there was plenty she wasn't telling him. Well, Hollis wasn't a criminal. She might have something to hide, but the police chief really didn't need to worry about that. There was probably plenty for him to do without making a special call to see if she was all right.

So, was he just checking up on a citizen, or did he actually want to speak to her about something? Hollis nearly gasped. Did he *know*?

"You're sure everything's good?"

Sure, she was hiding something, but it's not like she had any control over it. Conroy definitely figured something was wrong. But, she wasn't able to tell him if she wanted to keep her stepdad from being killed. Hollis had to continue to believe that whoever kidnapped Frankie was deadly serious. She needed to act like they meant every word of this dangerous deception, and had every intention of carrying out their threats if necessary.

Otherwise she could be needlessly jeopardizing his life for her own selfish gain, something that would make her just like everyone else. All the people she was trying to get away from. Not that people anywhere else were selfless. She didn't believe that. Everyone just did what they wanted, and if it looked like they actually cared, then there was always a hidden motive. Some way they'd gain from it. Always.

With new people, in a new town, she wouldn't have to care —or deal with unmet expectations—any longer. The people in Last Chance were part of her life. Her history. It had only complicated things.

That wasn't going to happen again. She wouldn't allow it.

Hollis straightened her shoulders and clutched the envelope

to her front. "Everything is fine, Conroy. Thanks." Since she had no idea why he was even here, she said, "Did you...need something?"

He'd never visited her at home before. In the diner, when he'd come in by himself or recently with his fiancé, he was cordial enough and would ask how she was. But then, everyone did that. Who actually meant it? Certainly no one she'd met before. Especially not the few disastrous times she'd gone to the church in town.

But she couldn't get dragged down into remembering all that. She had to figure out what the kidnappers wanted, and how to save her father.

Perhaps Conroy knew about the kidnapping and knew she couldn't say anything to him, but had come here to let her know that he wanted to help. Or that he was "on it," as those cops always said on TV. She'd watched enough crime dramas and missing persons shows to know she wasn't going to trust anyone —let alone the kidnappers. But she also couldn't risk Frankie's life on an assumption.

What was she supposed to do?

Hollis had no idea. And she was afraid that if she stood here talking to Conroy, eventually it would just slip out without her realizing. Then she wouldn't be able to take it back.

The police would be involved, and it would put Frankie's life in immediate danger. Or, more immediate than it already was.

Everyone loved Frankie. He was that "good ole boy" people loved to hang out with. Probably because things never got deeper than that. Just "surface" talk. Light. Easy. Even after the accident, it was like he'd convinced himself that things were still good. No problem.

This situation was anything but that.

But she needed answers. So Hollis said, "Do you know?" very quietly, in case someone was watching, or listening.

"Do I know what, Hollis?"

She bit her lip. He was going to make this hard? She shook her head. "I can't tell you."

"If you're in trouble I can help."

She wanted to shake her head again, but what was the point? What was the point in any of this? It was about Frankie, not the police chief making himself feel better by checking on her. Or whatever this was. She had no idea, since he'd never done this before.

She said, "Don't worry about it. I'll figure it out."

"So, there's something to figure out." Conroy studied her. "Tell me what's happening, Hollis. Maybe I can help."

"You can't. I have to do this by myself." Hopefully with a little help from her mom, though that was a long shot. What she didn't need was Conroy being overly nosy and inserting himself into the situation. Alerting the kidnappers.

"Maybe you wanna think about that? Give it some time. Let me know if you need something?"

She shook her head then. "I'm good."

His expression indicated he didn't believe her. He was a good cop, and a smart guy, so she wasn't entirely surprised at that. It wasn't like Hollis would be able to deceive him and get away with it. She appreciated that the police department here was solid. Good people, doing good things.

Which was why she didn't belong here.

She turned to the door. "I'll be fine."

It hurt to step away from him when she'd rather reach out, but this was for Frankie. She wanted to grab him and wail at how unfair it all was. She only wanted to leave, and now she had to stick around longer? She needed to read the note in the envelope and find out what she was supposed to do to get Frankie back.

Conroy was just slowing her down. Dropping by like this, unannounced. It could only be interpreted as suspicious. He was fishing for information she couldn't give him.

It had always been easier to push people away rather than

trust them. This was no different. Hollis had been solving her own problems every day of her life, with no help from anyone else. Every time she'd ever reached out to someone for help, her hand had been slapped back.

Why would things be different now?

She glanced over her shoulder at Conroy, now walking back to his car. Talking on his phone. Calling someone—probably about her. She sighed and watched him leave.

That was better. She was doing the right thing to not involve him. *Frankie.* His life was in danger, and there was nothing the police could do to help.

Hollis let herself in her apartment, all cleaned up and ready for her to leave. Ready for the new tenant to move in. She'd already told the manager she was done. That she wouldn't be here tomorrow.

Now she was going to have to take that back. Or move into the bed and breakfast.

How long would this take? Long enough for her to get Frankie back, but the money she'd set aside to start her new life somewhere else would quickly run out. She felt bad thinking about money. About herself. But why not? Everyone was selfish. Everyone lived in their own head, and did everything for themselves. Why should she do any differently?

She was already sticking around to get him back. So what if she only did that so she could leave without feeling guilty? If she rescued him, then Frankie could recover the money she'd spent. He'd like that. Compensation—or recompense. He wouldn't have to thank her. He could just cut her a check for what it had cost her.

She could leave. He could go back to his business.

Everyone would move on.

She closed the door to her apartment, then checked out the window and watched as Conroy pulled away. Hollis wanted to run after him. No. This was for the best.

No matter what, she would be alone. That was just the way it was going to be.

She opened the envelope, leaving the flash drive where it was. She pulled out the note and tried to ignore the way her hands shook.

PLUG THIS FLASH DRIVE INTO THE COMPUTER AT THE DINER AND COPY THE FILES TO THE HARD DRIVE.

Hollis sniffed. Copy files over. That was all she had to do, and the man who'd been a father to her would be returned?

How could she guarantee they would actually keep their word? This was going to involve a lot of trust from her. Blind faith was something she'd never been a fan of. What she wanted was proof, but would they kill him just because of her asking? Or hurt him more than he'd already been hurt? The man had suffered two broken legs in an accident. After that, there had been multiple surgeries.

How much more could he handle before he just…gave up?

Hollis pulled out her phone.

I GOT YOUR NOTE.

She wandered through the house. But with nothing to do, it was only aimless pacing. Until her phone beeped. She strode back to it and snatched it up.

DO IT OR HE DIES.

4

Will's first thought was that he couldn't move. He blinked, realizing at once that he was in an office and he was tied to a chair. *Not good.*

He blinked. Hollis's office at the diner? He'd been in the back hall one night when he picked her up and drove her home because her car had been in for an oil change. But she hadn't shown him the office.

Two men were in the room, their backs to him as they rifled through drawers at the desk and the file cabinet. Jeans. Beat-up jackets, and dirty hair. Rough-looking guys, but he figured he could take them both on if he had to. Neither of the guys had powered on the ancient desktop PC.

Will didn't move, or make a sound. Otherwise it would clue them in to the fact he was awake. Not something they needed to know. At least not until he was ready for them to know it.

He'd never met them before, but until they turned and he got good looks at their faces, he couldn't be a hundred percent sure. Still, they didn't seem familiar.

Didn't mean he hadn't met plenty of their type before, though.

Will's head ached. He wanted to moan but swallowed the

urge to make noise. He blew out a breath silently, letting his expression wash with all the pain he wanted to express out loud. His hands were tied securely to the swivel office chair. If he moved too much, he'd start spinning around. So, he sat tight, and if they came close enough, he would use his feet to keep them at bay while he figured out how to break free of the chair.

He shifted enough to confirm that they'd relieved him of his gun, which he didn't see on the desk or anywhere else.

One of the men turned. Will made like he was waking up.

"He's coming around."

Will blinked. He didn't recognize the voice, or the face. "Who…" He squeezed his eyes shut for a second, then said, "What's going on?"

The first guy, the only one who'd spoken so far, kept searching the file cabinet. His friend circled the desk to stand in front of Will.

"Let me go."

The man studied Will. Not sure what to make of him? Then he pulled a wallet off the desktop that Will hadn't previously noticed, and opened it. "Phil Tilley."

"Why'd you tie me up?" He groaned. "Did you knock me out? My head is *pounding*."

"Yeah…" The man dragged the word out. "I'm thinking Phil Tilley isn't your name. Just a real good alias. Considering I have good information you're actually an FBI agent."

"What are you talking about?" Will shook his head, then winced. It did actually hurt. That, he didn't have to pretend. "Phil. Tilley. Insurance agent."

"Mmm. I see the business card. Too bad for you my information is *good*. In fact, there's no one better."

A mole in the police department, maybe. Or West was seriously connected. If Hollis had found out that Phil was, in fact, an FBI agent, then it was since the last time he'd seen her.

Now he was blown.

Despite what these guys thought, he wasn't going to admit to anything. But to himself, he could admit that his cover was done. Bad guys in town knew he was an FBI agent.

"Which means it's legit, Mr. Special Agent."

Was that what Eric had been calling about? Trying to tell him he'd been blown?

"Guess you caught me." Will chuckled. "An FBI agent. That's priceless. Fighting crime, taking out bad guys." He full out laughed then, trying to make it sound real.

Probably he should have picked up when his handler had called, instead of sending Eric to voicemail. Then he'd have gotten a heads-up about this.

Live and learn, I guess.

Still, if Eric had told him he'd been blown, Will wouldn't have actually done anything different. Not really. He'd still have come in here; he just might have gone about it another way.

Will continued, "Now I'm sending West scrambling to hit back at me before I can get the chance to take her down." He waited for the reaction.

The guy's eyes flared.

Will realized he'd exposed his theory. "Yeah, I know all about her. Unless I'm not at the top of the food chain?"

He needed the information. Either he'd be arresting Hollis, even though he didn't really want to. Or she'd be testifying against the person who was *actually* responsible for everything that'd happened the past few months.

People terrorized. Threatened. Lives in danger.

The town itself had changed, along with the people who lived here. But Will wasn't a resident, so it wasn't like he cared. He wouldn't be around long enough to see how it played out.

"Mmm." The guy tossed his wallet on the desk. "Got the evidence you need, yeah? Or not. Because you're still here, and no arrests have been made. Which means you don't know squat."

"If I'm wrong, then prove it."

The guy grinned. Then he spun to his friend. "Find anything yet?"

"No. Might not be here."

"If it isn't, we need to know."

"Right." The friend went back to the file cabinet and its drawers stuffed with papers.

What were they looking for? Will needed them to admit who they worked for. What they were doing here. Something he could use to move forward when the time came. And that time had better be soon, or he was going to have a problem.

Eric would want to pull him out immediately if he'd really been blown. It was too hard to control who knew what information and who didn't, at least enough to contain any potential fallout. Will's op would be over. But when there was another layer beyond what the cops had found, more going on in Last Chance than anyone had even realized, no way was Will going to admit defeat and leave.

"Tell me who you work for."

The guy said, "Think you're going to interrogate me, and I'll just give up my boss to you?"

"It's worth a try." Will shrugged one shoulder. "What are you going to do with me anyway?"

"Good question." He stretched his arms the way Will desperately wanted to do and gave a flash of hairy stomach when his T-shirt rode up over his belt. "Haven't decided whether to kill you straight, or have some fun first."

"How about you put me out of my misery before you put me out of my misery?"

The guy barked a laugh.

"And tell me who you work for."

The guy grinned as he folded his arms. "West. Obviously."

That was supposed to give him something? "How does Hollis fit into this? She's involved, right?" Otherwise why would they be here? "Is she really West? Cause I heard she was. I didn't all the way believe it, but it could be true. Right?"

"Full of all kinds of surprises, that one." The guy studied him. "Found herself right in the middle of all this."

"So, what are you guys looking for here?"

The guy angled his head back to his friend but didn't take his attention from Will. "Think we should just tell him?"

"Put him out of his misery, before we put him out of his misery?" The friend chuckled. "Stupidest thing I've ever heard."

Will gritted his teeth. He tugged against the ties securing his hands, but there was nothing he could do about it. He was tied to the chair. No quick jump up to attack this guy's smug face and maybe get out of here afterwards. They'd have to cut him free first.

The guy in front of him swung out with his fist and nailed Will in the cheekbone before he could blink.

He hissed out a breath before he even tried to move his jaw. *Ouch.*

"You think I'm gonna spill everything?" His face reddened. "Like I'm some kind of idiot that doesn't know how to kill you dead? You think you're getting out of this when you *are not*. Welcome to your last rites, Special Agent Briar. You're a dead man. You just don't know it yet."

Will swallowed. His cheek bone hurt like the guy's fist was still against it. He squeezed his eyes shut.

No. This wasn't over.

Not by a long shot.

"You aren't going to kill me."

The guy laughed.

This had to go in his favor. It had to net him some results, otherwise he might as well let them kill him.

"Tied to a chair. Thinks he has the upper hand." The guy shook his head. "Did you find it yet?"

Before his friend could answer, Will said, "What are you looking for? Phil is dating Hollis. I can help you."

The two men shared a look.

Will said, "I can get you information. Unless you spread it

wide that I'm FBI." He shrugged, hoping he didn't sound desperate. "I can work for you guys. Pass you information. When the FBI sweeps up everyone connected to West, I can make a deal. Get you guys probation. No jail time. What do you say?"

"Seems to me like you don't know much. What could you possibly pass to me?"

Will gritted his teeth against the insinuation. "You think having an FBI agent in your pocket isn't going to come in handy?" Never mind what he knew, or didn't. This wasn't about his ability to do his job. Or his intelligence. "I'll think about it." But the guy got his cell from his jeans pocket and typed on the screen. Texting West?

"You do that. Because killing me is going to bring down a world of hurt. The FBI will never stop looking for you, and there won't be a place you can hide. They'll find you. You'll die, or you'll go to jail for the rest of your life. You won't get away with this." He knew he sounded desperate now, but he was running out of options.

The friend slid the file cabinet shut and turned. "There's nothing here."

"Still." The guy in front of him narrowed his eyes. "Just in case."

His friend chuckled.

"Go get the gasoline."

Will watched him leave. "You're gonna give up a prime opportunity to get ahead of the cops?"

"He's already ahead of the cops."

"And Hollis?"

"You don't need to worry about her. You'll be dead, and she'll just…disappear." He grinned.

When his friend returned with two gas cans—full, given the way he carried them—both guys started pouring it around the room. On the desk. Around Will.

Fumes licked up to his nose. Will shook his head. "Don't do this."

They were going to burn him alive? He'd rather get shot first but didn't want to ask for that. Who would?

The friend trailed out of the room and down the hall, leaving him with the first guy.

"Don't do this."

"I do enjoy when people beg." He grinned. "But unfortunately, we can't leave loose ends. That means the paperwork, and that means *you*."

"Don't—"

He walked out. Will's chest rose and fell rapidly. His body reacting to the fear before the rest of him even caught up. He gasped for air and looked around.

What was he supposed to do?

Fumes filled his nostrils.

God… He couldn't ask for help. Not even when he was about to die. God wasn't going to answer a guy like him.

He heard the whoosh of flames and started to push the chair back with his feet. He moved far enough, his bound hands hit the wall. The door that led to the bathroom.

Just as the room erupted into flames.

5

The second Hollis opened the door of her car, she smelled the smoke. *Fire.* She ran from her spot in the tiny rear parking lot to the back door, pulling her keys from her purse as she ran. But the door was ajar.

Her footsteps stammered to a stop as she realized smoke poured out the open doorway. The inside of the diner was on fire.

Hollis gasped, then had to cough as the smoke smell hit the back of her throat. She dropped her purse and the contents spilled out, but she didn't bother gathering it all back up.

The diner was burning.

She spun to face the car. *Her phone.* She needed to call 911; get firefighters here. Which meant the police would show up as well.

But the kidnapper's note. Hollis had the flash drive tucked in her purse. She needed to put the flash drive in the port on her office computer and copy the files over. Whatever they were and whatever information they contained, she had no idea. And it didn't matter. Doing it would save Frankie's life, and that was all that counted.

Hollis had no choice.

She pushed open the back door. At the far end of the hall, she could see flames through the thick smoke. The smell was awful. Thankfully no one was inside, or they'd be having a serious problem right now. No one could breathe that for long.

But her problem was clear.

She had to get to the office—assuming it wasn't full of fire as well—and get the flash drive into the computer before firefighters showed up, barring her from the office for days.

Frankie didn't have that long.

Hollis had no idea if the kidnappers would wait. Or what they'd do in the meantime. Kill him. Hurt him even more when he was already clearly in so much pain every day. The accident had turned a distant man into a surly, distant one. The last couple of years hadn't been easy, but she hadn't given up taking care of him—even if sometimes all he'd let her do was watch him struggle to do everything himself. That is, before he would eventually kick her out of his house at the end of the visit.

It wasn't like she would give up on him now. If she was going to do that, then she would've done it a long time ago.

Hollis pulled the flash drive from the spilled contents of her purse and stuck it in her jacket pocket. Then she jogged around the building to the left side where the office window was. She could see flames inside, through the blinds. She grasped the frame in order to pull the screen off the window. It pressed into her fingertips painfully. She hissed out a breath and got it free. It fell to the ground.

She didn't bother looking at her fingers. Who cared?

This was much more important than her own comfort.

"Argh!"

Hollis glanced in the direction of the sound. A man, crying out. She moved to the next window—the Jack and Jill bathroom with entrances from both the office and the hallway.

"Argh!"

She heard him again. There was someone in there. And whoever he was needed help.

This window was a whole lot smaller than the other diner windows, but big enough for someone to stand on the back of the toilet and climb out.

Hollis grabbed a rock from the ground and slammed it against the frosted glass. It took her a couple of tries to break the glass, then she had to break all the corner pieces. Shards dropped toward her, but she ignored it. Even when one disappeared down the collar of her shirt.

She winced and kept going.

"Who's there?"

She knew that voice. "Phil?" What was her boyfriend doing in there? "Are you in the bathroom?"

"Yes. I'm so glad you're here, Hollis." He sounded so relieved it rushed through her, a surge of gratitude. "But I can't get out! I'm tied up. I need help."

She didn't want to grasp the window frame with the jagged glass. Hollis looked around. What was... A tire. She hefted it over, then rolled it to the wall. She stood on it, gaining six or so inches in height. Enough to look over the ledge, through the window and into the bathroom.

"Phil?"

He winced.

"What happened?" He looked like he had blood on his face. Like he'd been beaten. He was also laying on his side, his arms awkwardly behind his back. "Why are you tied up?"

Instead of answering her question, he said, "Can you find something to cut me free?"

She was going to have to climb in there after all. "Yeah. Wait one second." As if he had the means to be someplace else at the moment.

Hollis raced back to her purse, fell to her knees on the grass, and rummaged. She found her nail clippers. Hopefully they would work. Then she ran back to the window.

She heard sirens in the distance and muttered a thank you to whoever was listening. Her beliefs weren't something she'd considered much. Church had been a disaster. She just didn't fit there in that culture.

It was fine. They didn't want her either, so she hadn't gone back.

How she felt about God was different than how she felt about the culture, she could admit that. But she could also admit that He might use his people to speak for Him, regardless of her opinion or whether or not they accurately represented who God was.

So maybe, if He was really up there, He didn't want her. Maybe. Deep down, she knew He would still be God, with the ability to make things happen down here, regardless.

Hollis pushed aside the thoughts and focused. She had to haul her body up and over the window ledge, so she pulled off her jacket and put it over the sill where the broken glass was. Wincing at the fact she was ruining her favorite new accessory splurge, she climbed into the window—narrowly avoiding landing her foot in the toilet.

She wasn't a small woman. Never had been, and never would be. She ran a few times a week. But she also ate whatever she wanted, whenever she wanted to. Because life was *way* too short to feel guilty about food that tasted so good. Anyway, Phil hadn't seemed to care about her size. It wasn't like he was a small man. He was so big, he almost made her feel dainty.

"I have nail clippers." She held them up, between her fingers.

"Worth a try." Phil shifted so she could see his hands.

Hollis stepped over his legs. There wasn't much room in the bathroom. She crouched and tried to snip the ties holding his hands, part of her weight on the chair. She needed to hurry up. His clothing was damp, and he smelled like gasoline. The air in the bathroom was getting thicker. "Is the fire going to spread in here?"

"If it does, I hope we're outside at the time."

She figured that meant he wanted her to go as quickly as possible. "Almost there. What about the office? Can I go in there?"

"If there's something in there you want to save, I'm sorry to say you are out of luck."

His arms shifted, and he tugged at the ties. Hollis cut, and he pulled, enough the ties broke apart. Phil rolled and stood up in one smooth move. She'd always liked the way he moved. He just had…presence. It was easy to get swept up in the way he commanded everything around him, the force of who he was seemed to hang in the air.

He held out his hand and pulled her to her feet, then didn't let go as he moved to the window. "Go. You first."

Hollis looked at the door to the office. She needed to get the flash drive in the computer. It was what she had to do to save Frankie. Who knew when she'd get another chance? Or how long it would take her to get him back before she could finally do what she'd planned and leave town for good.

"Come on."

"I need to—"

He grasped her arm and gently tugged. "Whatever it is, leave it."

She stepped on the closed toilet lid, hauled herself back up, and climbed out. With a little help from Phil.

She jumped down onto the gravel. She still had the flash drive at least.

"Good thinking with your jacket." He landed beside her.

"I hope it's not ripped. I *love* this jacket." She pulled it from the window frame and looked at it. Like the condition of her leather jacket was the point here. She held it to her front. "Are you okay?"

"Thanks to you." He leaned close and pressed a kiss to her cheek. "Thank you. You might've saved my life."

"Oh. Well." She pressed her hand against the jacket, feeling for the flash drive. Where had she put it? Which pocket was she feeling, the left or the right? She needed to—

"Hollis! Will!"

She frowned as Sergeant Basuto ran toward them. Conroy came after him. The sergeant wore his uniform, and the chief, his customary suit. Both their expressions portrayed serious concern. She felt the same. Not only was the diner likely destroyed, but she still needed to do what she had to in order to get Frankie back.

Conroy said, "You okay, Briar?" But he was looking at Phil.

Before she could correct him on Phil's name, he looked at her. "Are you okay, Hollis?"

"Yes, you—"

Phil cut her off. "Two guys tied me up and set fire to the place."

Conroy frowned. "Can you ID them?"

"Yeah."

Sergeant Basuto slapped Phil on the back. "Never a dull moment for the FBI, am I right?"

Hollis frowned. What was he talking… She took a breath, and had to cough it out. "I need to—"

Phil cut her off *again*. "EMTs?"

Conroy nodded. "You should both get checked out."

The men glanced at each other. Hollis saw there was something they weren't telling her. "What is it?"

Maybe they knew something about Frankie that Conroy hadn't wanted to say earlier.

She turned to Phil. "I'm so sorry someone tied you up and hurt you." This weirdness had to be about everything that was going on.

He winced. "I'm good. Let's go get checked out, okay? We both inhaled a lot." He reached for her.

Hollis took a step back. "Not until you tell me what's going on. Is it Frankie?"

Conroy frowned. "What makes you think this is about your stepdad?"

"I…" She didn't know what to say. "There are things I need to do. In my office." Hollis waved at the building. "I need to know when I can get in there. *As soon* as I can get in there."

He nodded. "I'll let you know."

"Thank you, Chief."

Conroy dipped his head to the side. "Let's go, Basuto." Then he said, "You guys, right behind us."

Phil said, "Copy that."

Words she'd never heard him say before. She twisted to face him straight on then and saw he wore jeans and a sweater with buttons at the collar and long sleeves that showed the muscle definition in his biceps. She'd never seen him in anything like it before. He always wore slacks and button-down shirts with a pen in the breast pocket. Now he looked…rougher. And not just because he'd been soaked with gasoline and pushed around. Though that definitely contributed.

"Phil," she began.

He winced.

"What?"

"We need to go see the EMTs."

At the end of the building, two firefighters rounded the corner. "Heard you were here," one called out. "You okay, Briar?"

"Yeah. We're good."

She frowned at Phil's words and glanced between him and the first responder. "What is—"

"My name isn't Phil Tilley. That's just an alias I've been using so I don't have to be a biker all the time. Not that there's anything wrong with being a biker. I just wanted to be someone…nice for a while. Not Hammer."

"What are you talking about?"

"My name is Will Briar." He paused for a second. "I'm an FBI Special Agent here undercover."

And he'd...

This man had...

Whatever had overcome Hollis during the visit with her mom—whatever had caused her to swipe her mom's glass from her hand and shatter it—showed up again.

She lifted her hand, open palm, and slapped him across the cheek.

6

"Hollis!"

She didn't stop. Just kept going, moving with long strides down the side of the diner toward the front, her purse swinging against her hip.

Will pushed out a long breath. His head pounded, and his throat felt like he'd swallowed a packet of razor blades. Every exhale brought with it a coughing jag.

"You okay?"

Will waved off the firefighter and bent forward. He laid his hands on his knees and coughed until he'd gotten the phlegm out, then spat. As he straightened, something snagged his attention over by where Hollis's purse lay on the ground.

A flash drive.

He pocketed it and then went after her, ignoring what that said about him—considering she was the chief suspect in his criminal conspiracy case. The one in which everyone else was either dead or missing, and he had little to no evidence. But he still wasn't going to give up. Will didn't do that.

Especially when he'd come up against a woman as good as she was at pulling the wool over everyone's eyes.

He'd half expected Conroy to apologize to her. Will was the

one who'd been tied up and beaten, then nearly burned alive. Hollis had rescued him. Which pretty much just proved his point. Regardless of how Conroy forced the people who worked for him to prove themselves, as evidenced by the way he demanded they get him everything he needed wrapped up in a neat bow, Will wasn't going to submit to that.

Ask his FBI handler. Will rarely submitted to anything.

Then there was Hollis. So much concern on her face, even when she'd probably known exactly why he'd been there.

"Hey." The EMT stepped in front of him.

Will pulled up short. "I'm..." He tried to finish with, "fine" but had to cough half a dozen times.

"You're fine?"

Will pressed his lips together and made a face.

The EMT chuckled. A woman, and she had a nice laugh. Beyond her, Hollis sat at the edge of the ambulance. The other EMT was looking at her elbow.

All while she glared daggers at him.

"Let's take a look at you."

"That's all I need." Certainly not a hospital visit. Not when he had Hollis right there in his grasp, and it would be so easy to get a confession out of her.

"You're not the one who gets to decide that. I get it that all you alpha types are the same, but if there's reason to take you in, I will."

She walked him all the way to the ambulance and Hollis shifted to the side. Will climbed in, followed by the female EMT. He sat on the stretcher, and the EMT knelt beside him, using her gloved fingers to feel around his face. He took her hand and put it on the spot where he'd been hit, on the back of his head. She met his gaze, something in her expression, like interest.

Will felt nothing in return.

Phil had been slightly besotted by Hollis, so that wasn't surprising. Will looked at Hollis now as she sat on the edge of the open doors, and she turned to look at him. She'd clearly seen him touch the EMT, and the look they shared.

Or there was another reason she now looked disgusted by him.

He called over to her, "We both know there wasn't any more between you and I than simple attraction. It isn't like it was a serious thing between us."

They'd dated for only a few weeks, didn't talk much, and never deeply. They hadn't shared those important things that couples should.

Though, given his relationship history—and any he'd seen in real life outside Last Chance—Will didn't exactly know how it was supposed to go. But he knew that Phil and Hollis hadn't had anything more than a lukewarm attraction.

"Whatever you need to tell yourself to justify the fact that you lied to me." She turned away from him.

"*I'm* the one that lied?"

The woman was hiding her involvement in a criminal empire, and she wanted to give him a hard time about being one of the good guys? So, he hadn't been able to tell her his true identity. So what? That was part of the job. He wasn't supposed to get romantically involved. But could you call a few dates and a couple of chaste kisses involvement? He didn't.

Whatever you need to tell yourself. Her words rang between his ears. Warning bells he didn't like hearing much.

"I have no idea what you're insinuating," she said, "but considering I told you from the beginning that my name is Hollis—my real name—I think I'm entitled to be offended. Mr. FBI Special Agent." He could tell there was more she wanted to say. She shook her head. "Guess now I know why it felt like you were holding back."

He snorted. If there had been any of that happening, it was from the woman hiding a criminal enterprise. After all, she'd pretended she was interested in him. Why do that if it wasn't in order to continue the ruse? Get nice Phil Tilley, poor unsuspecting traveling insurance salesman, into a relationship so that no one would think she was up to any illegal activity.

The entire diner had the stink of money laundering all over it. No way could she sustain a business on breakfast and lunch alone and manage to pay all her employees the good salary she gave them. And, on top of that, he heard she'd given a young, single mom in town two grand a couple of months ago. Just as a gift, to help her through a rough patch.

He just needed to prove his suspicion.

There was no point dwelling on how soundly he'd been played. Love didn't come without earning it. He should've known it was all a ruse when she'd accepted his invitation for that first date straight out, never once making him work for it. But he'd been too stupid to figure it out.

She'd probably even sent those men to her diner just to throw him off her trail.

Will said, "You need to come to the police station and answer some questions about who might've gone through your office, and what they were looking for."

She sputtered. Before she could say anything, Conroy appeared beside the EMT who was looking at the palm of her hand. The police chief said, "He's right. We need a statement."

"I thought it just caught fire."

Will said, "They poured gasoline on me."

She gasped, shooting him a look of concern. It was too late for that. He knew what she was up to. Trying to act all sympathetic wasn't going to work. *Fool me once.* He was the pro at this, not her. Will had been working undercover for years. There were few better than him. He'd more than proven his worth to the FBI. But still, in a lot of ways, it felt like there was so much more of a mark for him to carve out. Continue making a name for himself.

"Will needs to ID the men that did this," Conroy said, "and I'd like you to look at the pictures."

"Okay." Her voice sounded small. "I'll drive over there."

Conroy nodded. Will started to object, since letting her out of his sight didn't sit well with him. The chief shot him a look and shook his head.

Will swallowed. He was working with the Last Chance Police Department at their invitation. If he screwed up the relationship by pushing too hard, he would lose the standing he had.

Hollis pulled on her jacket and walked off. Conroy watched her.

The EMT handed over an ice pack. "Nice...your friend."

Will didn't care what she thought. "You obviously know nothing about her." He climbed out of the ambulance and touched the ice pack to the back of his head.

He felt Conroy's eyes on him.

"What?"

Conroy shook his head. "Nothing. I'm driving."

That was fine with Will. He could get a ride and pick up his car later. He felt in his pockets for his phone and realized he had left it back in his car. His fingers closed around his keys and the flash drive he should've already given back to Hollis.

Though, technically, he didn't know that he actually needed to give it back to Hollis at all. It had been on the ground. Maybe she dropped it out of her purse, or when she bent to pick up her stuff. Or maybe someone else had dropped it. He didn't know for sure that it was hers. Might belong to anyone, for all he knew.

Will shut his eyes all the way to the police station, just so he'd have a few minutes to collect his thoughts and Conroy wouldn't feel the need to talk to him.

When they pulled into the chief's parking spot, he half expected Hollis's car to not be there. But it was.

Will strode into the entrance lobby. Hollis broke off her conversation with Kaylee who worked the front desk. Usually she was cordial. Today she looked like she wanted to spit fire at him.

Hollis didn't look much happier than that. "Will, is it? Will Briar."

"That's my name."

"The one your mother gave you."

Will shrugged. "Let's get inside, where we can get some water."

"Coffee would be good."

Conroy came up behind them. "Coffee does sound good. Kaylee?"

She hopped off the stool. "On it."

Will led the way to the empty desk he'd used a couple of times. He needed to talk to Eric, tell him he'd been made—which the FBI agent probably already knew. He also needed to tell his FBI handler that his gun had been stolen. It wasn't his duty weapon, but they didn't want a gun given to an undercover agent to show up who knows where. Used in the commission of a crime.

Not good PR for the bureau. And something he tried to avoid.

"You're really sticking with this?"

Will looked up at Conroy, standing beside the desk.

"She saved your life."

"I can be grateful, but I don't owe her."

Conroy shook his head and wandered to his office. Probably planning to call Eric and tell him all about how Will continued to be a monumental screw up. People did that a lot, mostly in small towns like this. Usually because they lacked the patience to see what he came up with.

Will had to move fast.

Before he pulled up the local mug shot database and looked for those two men, he plugged the flash drive in.

Hollis set a mug beside him.

He glanced up at her, much like he'd done with Conroy. She pulled over a chair. When she sat, she put both hands in her lap.

Her chin was set. Determined not to let on how she was really feeling.

Because he'd figured her out, and she knew it.

"Thank you."

She sipped her own drink and said nothing.

He told the computer he wanted to look at the files on the flash drive. "Any idea why someone would be rooting through your file cabinets and desk drawers?"

She shook her head. "I probably had half a pack of gum in there."

"I doubt they were looking to freshen their breath, Hollis."

"I know that, Will. I'm not stupid. They *burned down* the diner."

He wanted to reach out and touch her hand, but didn't. "I'm sorry."

The flash drive loaded. Will clicked through the folders and found a bunch of PDF documents. He pulled up the first one, an invoice for new napkins for the diner. The total price was twenty-four thousand dollars and was dated last month.

"How often do you purchase napkins for the diner?"

"That's a weird question, but I'll bite." She said, "Every two months or so."

"At twenty-four thousand dollars?"

She lowered her mug before she even took a sip. "How much?"

"You think I'm stupid, don't you?"

Hollis started to speak.

"No. Don't bother. Even I know napkins don't cost that much. What you likely *don't* know that I know, is how businesses can hide money laundering in purchases so everything looks above board. Bonus, you can write off the expense. It's a win-win. Right?"

He clicked the next file and felt his eyebrows rise. She had a vendor receipt that proved she'd been in the city when an illegal deal went down, which also meant he could place her in the vicinity. If that didn't scream, "proof" she was West, then he didn't know what would. "Conroy!"

The chief hung up his phone and came out of his office. "Is there a reason you're screaming across this office, Special Agent Briar?"

"I just thought you'd want to know." Will stood and pulled out a set of cuffs. "I'm arresting Hollis for criminal conspiracy."

7

Hollis gasped. She stood up so fast the chair rolled backward, and she heard it hit the desk behind. "What are—"

He was around the desks and in front of her before she could finish, lifting one of her hands and slapping a cold metal cuff on it with a clink.

"Phil—"

He snapped the other on. "It's Will."

"You know what I mean." She shook her head. "What are you doing?"

Her hands were cuffed in front of her now. *Arrested.* This was crazy. What on earth? One second she was preparing to give a statement, and then all of a sudden, the very next second, she had cuffs on.

"I was almost fooled." As he spoke, the cops in the room stood listening. "But this proves the truth." Will pointed at the monitor where he'd been sitting. "A flash drive with your financial records."

"Mine?"

"The diner's invoices." His face was hard, his eyes devoid of any kind of emotion. "Proof you're hiding money in the receipts, showing the IRS all the money you've spent and written off as expenses."

"To fund my lavish lifestyle?"

He'd been to her apartment. He knew what kind of car she drove. Exactly what was she doing with these ill-gotten gains? While she stared at him, pleading for him to see the truth, her heart was breaking. She would never let him see it, though. Hollis couldn't ever, even for one second, let him in on how she felt.

If she did that, he would destroy her.

She'd really liked Phil. That was the worst of it.

While he'd been investigating her, Hollis hadn't had the first inkling he wasn't Phil Tilley, the guy she was seeing. He'd seemed so nice, and he'd been a perfect gentleman. Now she knew why. The FBI probably had rules about getting intimate with the suspect.

Meanwhile, Hollis had been getting to know him. Like a chump, she'd decided that though he was rough under that salesman veneer, she would fall for him. She'd actually *liked* that he wasn't so clean cut. She'd thought that made them a good fit, considering her past.

Hollis would have let him in. They'd been heading to a place where she would have brought him into her life fully. She'd have told him everything. *Heart. Breaking.* Or would she have? Her suitcase was packed. Ready to leave and walk away from him. Maybe deep down she'd known he wasn't telling her the truth.

That didn't matter now.

Will had blown through all that attraction. He was going to stomp on it. Brand her a criminal. Now he was arresting her. She had to get Frankie back. She had to leave.

Maybe that had been instinct protecting her all along.

It could be, on some level, she'd known he wasn't telling her everything. It would explain why she'd been preparing to walk away from him. A man she was attracted to and had thought was a good guy. That had to be it.

She'd known all along he wasn't telling her the truth. It didn't have anything to do with fear, or the fact she'd never let anyone else in. Hollis had simply known he was lying. Somehow.

He said, "You're taking cash from someone and laundering it through your business. Am I right?"

He was so far from wrong, it wasn't even funny. She opened her mouth to argue with him, but realized she didn't even know where to start.

"Nothing to say, I see." He kept staring at her with his injured face. He'd been beaten. Had they knocked a screw loose? Maybe there was a bleed in his brain, and it was causing him to think crazy thoughts when the truth was so obvious.

Still, his stare was unnerving. "No explanation." He glanced at his phone, then turned to Conroy. "My boss said to bring her in, along with the evidence."

A muscle jumped in Conroy's cheek.

"You're not going to say anything?" Hollis glanced around. "He's arresting me for being West. This is insane!"

"Let's go." Will picked up her purse and walked it back to retrieve the flash drive.

"Don't touch my things." Suddenly, she didn't want him touching any of her personal belongings. "Give me my purse. You don't get to touch my purse."

"So you can pull out a weapon, attack me, and escape?"

Kaylee gasped.

Hollis wanted to tell her everything was fine. But how could she? He really thought she had it in her to hurt him when he was already all banged up from those men at the office? Was that even real? She hadn't seen anyone leaving. Maybe he'd made all that up. Set the fire himself.

Before she could demand an explanation, Will said, "Conroy?"

The police chief retrieved a brown paper evidence bag and placed her purse inside, right before he rolled the top down and handed it to her.

She said, "Please don't do this."

Conroy didn't respond.

Will said nothing. He just took her arm and led her away from the police chief. She glanced back over her shoulder. They all just stood there.

Not one of them said anything in her defense.

The truth would come out, right? *Right.* Not with her track record. She was more likely to get convicted. It was better to face the facts—she was going to go to jail. The kidnappers would realize she hadn't done anything for them, and they would kill her. Hollis moaned. "Frankie."

Conroy said, "What about him?"

"You need to help Frankie."

She wanted to say more, but just then it occurred to her. *The flash drive.* That was where Will was getting his evidence. The files they wanted her to transfer to her office computer were ones that *incriminated* her as West. They'd wanted the evidence planted on her computer hard drive. Someone wanted her to take the fall as West and go to jail.

Will dragged her as far as the front door. She glanced back once and saw Kaylee crying. Conroy still standing there. The rest of them, staring.

They didn't even stop him.

Then she stumbled out, tugged along by an insistent Will and his long stride. A whimper escaped her lips, and the front door shut her off from the very people who were supposed to help the residents of Last Chance. The ones who should fight for the truth, and for justice.

And they just stood there.

Hollis was alone.

"Don't bother crying. It won't help you." He unlocked his car and loaded her into the front seat, depositing the brown paper bag in the back. She sat, stoic and silent, while he turned the engine on and pulled out. "I won't be swayed by your tears."

She could hardly believe this was happening. He was bound and determined to catch West, to such an extent that he was steamrolling right over her *and* her feelings. Crushing her heart in his wake as he raced toward a conviction. Was he really so determined to close this case? Probably so he could leave Last Chance and get away from her for good.

She didn't need a guy like that doing her any favors. The same way she'd never needed her mom to do her any, either. It was just further proof that everyone was only in this thing—life—for themselves. Everyone was the star in their own show, and people just trampled on others whenever they wanted to.

Which meant that if she was going to get out of this, it was going to be because she saved herself. No one else was going to help her.

She would have to tell the truth. But only in the right way, at the right time, to the right people. That was how the world worked. Honesty got you nowhere. She had to make a plan and be smart about this. Everyone knew trusting in the justice system got you convicted of a crime you didn't commit. Just another statistic of some over-zealous civil servant trying to make their quota, so they didn't lose their job.

Hollis squeezed her eyes shut. People like her never saw real justice.

That was why she had to figure this out. There were so many things she'd never told anyone, and had never planned to—until Phil. Now she'd have to work out what to say. About the past. Her mom. Frankie.

They really thought she was West?

Hollis would have to explain everything instead of leaving and starting over. Phil…that whole thing had been unexpected and way too tempting. Honestly, it was better to be done with it—with him—just as she'd planned. Not that finding out he was a liar was for the best. But she didn't have to worry about whether life would give her anything good. It wouldn't. Letting that hope finally die was for the best.

Now she knew his truth. Phil didn't even exist.

Hollis lifted her shoulder and wiped her cheekbone before the tear could fall.

"Why would you do this?" His voice was hard. He didn't sound hurt. On the contrast, her entire world was shattering.

Frankie would be dead, because she hadn't done what the kidnappers wanted.

She would be in jail.

He said, "You're a business owner. And yet you're caught up in money laundering? I don't get it, Hollis. I thought you were a good person."

She shifted in her seat so she could face him more fully. He really thought she was going to have a conversation with him right now. With her in cuffs. That they'd...what...*chat* on the way to his office? As if. Maybe he hoped she'd come clean to him, and he would be able to gloss over the part where he had arrested her to prove what he *thought* was true. No real proof. No benefit of the doubt.

Like finding proof would be possible when it was nothing but a fabrication.

She said, "I have no interest in speaking to you, so don't bother asking me any questions. When we get to your office, I'm going to be calling my lawyer. After that, I'm happy to speak to your boss. Not you."

She twisted back and stared out the side window.

As she'd told him to his face—the *liar*—Hollis had no interest in speaking with him. A man who would pretend to be attracted to her. She should've known. She'd thought he was sweet, but did she really think he would be attracted to a woman who looked like her? Obviously, it was all deception.

Her mom was right. She could never attract a man, let alone one who was an FBI agent. FBI agents were supposed to be good people. The heroic kind who protected the innocent and worked to see justice. Will didn't fit that mold. Then again, he did work as an undercover. That was all a lie, right? Maybe he wasn't the regular kind of FBI agent. More like a renegade.

Or he was a bad guy. He might even work for West, himself. This could all be misdirection. A way to solidify everyone's conclusion that she was the local crime lord. That was laughable, but it could be part of their plan.

What if the kidnappers did this all along? What if they'd worked it out so that she ended up with the flash drive, arrested? Maybe this was how it was supposed to go down. Frankie was leverage, and Hollis went down as West. She'd tried to do her part, and Will had improvised.

Was Will really working with West? The idea descended on her like a cold breeze. Hollis shivered in her seat.

Maybe he wasn't taking her to the FBI.

He could be taking her to West.

She gasped a split second before the world spun. Too late, Hollis realized a car had slammed into the back of Will's, on the side where she was sitting.

His car spun around in the road.

Hollis screamed. Even Will cried out. The car spun off the road and dipped down in a way that made her want to hurl. Before she could figure out how bad the situation might be, they were falling.

Falling.

Down.

The car slammed into something, and the world went black.

8

Will's chest hurt. Even breathing hurt. Like he'd been hit by—

He wheezed, trying to get air. Something was in his face. He batted it away, then realized it was a hand. Will was on his left side, smashed against the window. The whole car was on its side. *Hollis.*

He turned to look...up...at the passenger seat, while his brain tried to amass thoughts on what must've happened.

He choked out a moan. "Hollis."

She was suspended above him. While he assessed her position to figure out how to get both of them out, a drop of blood splatted down upon his cheek. Will wiped it away. "Hollis."

He pressed his lips together. It was probably better that she didn't regain consciousness right now. Better that he get her out of the car first.

The windshield was completely shattered. He lifted his leg, got his foot up above the dash and kicked the glass the rest of the way out, then scrambled upright. That put his face right by hers.

"Hollis." He whispered her name, pressing two fingers to her neck. Just in case. He felt the thump of her heart beating and there were no words to describe the way that tightness in his chest eased. *Don't leave me.*

It still hurt every time he breathed. Whiplash? Maybe. He'd been in car accidents before, and it always hurt more a day or two later. The next few days wouldn't be so fun.

Will unsnapped her seatbelt, and she tumbled down onto his lap. With his backside, he landed on the door handle with a wince, and for a second just sat there, feeling her in his arms. Will buried his face in her hair and inhaled. Not that he wanted to smell her. That would be weird. But in that second, he just needed to acknowledge—if only to himself—that they were both alive.

"Hollis."

She stirred in his arms, a low mewing sound that didn't seem right emitting from her. He shifted her and saw her hands were still cuffed. She moved one, the other stiff and awkward, like she was trying to hold it.

Will dug in his pocket for the cuff keys and set her free. He touched her cradled arm gently. Hollis let out a low moan, so he tucked it to her stomach which seemed to be better for her.

They had to get out of here.

He looked around for his phone, and then set Hollis down where he'd been sitting against the driver's door. She was still mostly unconscious. He should pull her out and lay her on the grass so when help got here, they could get to her more quickly.

He should call Dean.

No, Dean was busy these days. Calling 911 would suffice, and he had faith they'd definitely send the former Navy SEAL and unofficial town EMT, if he was closest. No one wasted resources in Last Chance.

Problem was, he couldn't find his phone.

Will climbed out to look around, palming his gun from the holster on his hip. But there was no holster. Actually, he hadn't seen his gun since he'd been knocked unconscious at the diner.

Not good. Did he have a concussion? He thought maybe he couldn't all the way think straight.

The car was flipped on its side in the ditch. The back, right quarter panel completely busted, tire shredded. The roof would be barely visible from the street.

He checked the area around the car. His wasn't the only phone, but Hollis's cell was in her purse—which she'd told him he couldn't get into. Were these extenuating circumstances? He didn't know how she'd feel about him rummaging through her purse, considering he'd cuffed her and was hauling her to the FBI only moments before.

"Will?"

It took him a second to absorb that she had been calling for him by his real name—and not by his moniker, Phil—before he moved back to the open window where he'd kicked out the windshield.

He crouched. "Hollis?"

She blinked, her gaze coming to focus on him. Then she shifted her arms and winced, crying out. "My arm really hurts." The one he'd noticed earlier. Now she held it against her.

He nodded, that sinking feeling rising. His cuffs had caused that. The same way his inattention had caused this crash.

"What happened?"

He was still looking around for his phone, but said, "A truck clipped the rear side of the car, and we spun off the road."

She took a breath and winced.

"Can you move?"

She nodded.

"I'm trying to find my phone."

"Where's mine?" Her voice sounded small and pained.

"Don't look for it. I'll see if I can get to the backseat." He climbed back for the evidence bag. "Is it okay if I go in there?" She'd seemed averse to it before. Out of pride, or because she had something to hide?

"Will."

He shifted back so she'd be able to see his face. "Yeah?"

She pressed her lips together.

Will gave her shoulder a squeeze. The animosity was gone now. He didn't think she was innocent, but no one could fake anything right now. Even the best actor or actress would struggle through the pain and shock she felt. He needed to be cautious, but he also had to make sure she didn't have some kind of medical turn for the worse. Will knew the signs of serious problems, but had no training beyond basic field medicine.

"It's not turning on." Her phone was a different model than his, but they weren't so different he didn't know how to start it up. "Could it be dead?"

She pushed out a breath. "Maybe. The battery isn't good. I should've replaced it." She didn't say more, and he saw her take a few long breaths.

She hadn't just spent the money to buy herself a new phone? Will watched her breathe. "You okay?"

"Other than wanting to hurl all over my lap, I feel like I got hit by a truck."

"We did." He wasn't going to sugar-coat it. Will should've realized, before they were struck, what was happening, but he hadn't. He'd failed. Now they were both bruised, and he needed to figure out a way to get aid to them. Or get them back to civilization.

"Help me out."

Will nodded, climbed out, and reached back to assist her as she fumbled her way out. She straightened, and he didn't let go of her elbow. Will had to resist the strong urge to gather her to him and give her a hug.

Meanwhile, she eyed him. "Why are you being so nice?"

Why would he not? "We were in a car accident together."

"Yeah, after you *arrested* me."

"If you hadn't done anything criminal, I wouldn't have."

"You have no idea what I've done and what I haven't." She moved out of reach and began to take careful steps around the car. There wasn't much room to move. Hollis went to the trunk end of the car, bent double, and deposited the contents of her stomach into the weeds.

"You okay?" He climbed the embankment. Not too many cars on the road, he heard the sound of an engine intermittently.

She made a noncommittal sound, and he replied with, "I'll flag someone down, then help you up."

Together they could hobble to a vehicle and hopefully get a ride into town. His foot slipped on the damp ground, and he slid back down, turning as he went, so that his feet hit the bottom of the embankment He was sitting down right where he started. Will blew out a breath.

Hollis was smiling at him. "Good one."

He figured that wasn't about her being impressed. More like amused by his attempt to climb. "Sit down or something, yeah?"

"Did you bring my purse out of the car?"

"No." He groaned. "I'll get it, but I really want to flag someone down."

"Well, I need a mint to get the taste of puke out of my mouth."

Will sighed. He climbed back into the car and got her belongings, setting the brown bag on the ground and tearing it open so she could fish out whatever she wanted one-handed. Hollis sat beside it and rummaged.

"Good?"

"Huh?" She looked up. "Oh. Yes, thank you."

Still determined to hide things from him? He had no idea what she wanted, or how she felt. He'd have to ask her later. Not that he cared. She needed to be in custody, preferably in one piece, even if that meant she was in cuffs at the hospital. He figured she needed at least a brace, if not a cast, on her arm. Was it broken or simply sprained?

Will had the flash drive in his jeans pocket, so it didn't matter what she did. He had the evidence he needed.

Sure, he had to ignore the pang he felt from acknowledging that someone he was attracted to, and so badly wanted to care for right now, was a criminal. He needed to get her to Eric. That was all. Special Agent Cullings would decide what to do with her. Will planned to call his dad and take a vacation while the charges were filed. He didn't want to be there.

This was hard enough. Will might have failed to realize in time that the truck intended to run them off the road. He wasn't going to fail to get her to the FBI.

"What are you looking for?"

"Apart from gum?"

He pressed his lips together.

"I thought you were getting help, Mr. FBI Hero."

What was that supposed to mean? It wasn't like he was a good guy. Why else would he be an undercover agent? All the straight-laced, clean-cut, Ivy League guys worked in their offices, taking down white-collar criminals. Will had never been that guy. He was the scholarship kid. The Army brat. He mostly figured they'd taken pity on him. Then they funneled him into undercover work, and he quickly figured out why.

He was too rough for the kind of work where he'd be visible to mainstream society. Will was much better suited to donning a persona and talking his way into gangs. Biker clubs. Mercenary groups. He'd been so many different people over the past ten years, he had no idea who he'd be if he went on vacation.

Will tried again to scramble up the embankment. It took a couple of attempts, but when he reached the top, he looked back at Hollis. Triumphant. She wasn't looking at him. She just sat there waiting for rescue. Looking around like this was a sightseeing trip, or she had all day to wait.

Maybe she did. He was the Fed here, and she was the criminal in custody. If he didn't take her in, she could escape. Hollis would probably disappear into the distance, and he'd never find her again.

Will would never know the truth.

He turned to see the area. A semi roared down the highway, too fast for him to wave his hand in time and get them to see. Who would stop for them? If he could get a phone, then he could call Conroy or Eric and get a ride here to pick them up.

A car engine turned on.

What? Will found the source of the sound. A blue car...one he'd seen before. Following them, right behind the truck that hit them. Two vehicles? He'd dismissed the idea at the time. After all, why would more than one car be in pursuit? That didn't make sense.

The blue compact inched toward him.

Will saw the gun barely in time. A shot cracked. He flung himself out of the way, but since the embankment dipped sharply, he wound up flying over the edge to land on the soggy grass at the bottom, beside their useless car.

Hollis's cry of alarm rushed in his ears. Will scrambled up and went to her, gathering her purse as he said, "We've gotta go."

He helped her up. She shook her head, glancing around. "What's going on?"

"They're still here, making sure we don't get out of here alive. And they have a gun." He shoved her to the far side of the embankment. "Go. We have to run."

9

One of her boots slipped down the incline. Hollis planted her knee, shifted her purse onto her shoulder, and scrambled up. Will's hands grasped her waist and together they crested the top.

A gunshot blew out a chunk of tree to her left.

Hollis squealed. She lifted her working arm to shield her head and they ran.

"Go right."

She responded to Will's order as fast as she could, so thankful she'd forced herself to exercise every day after she got off work the last year or so. Otherwise she would probably already be dead. They should put that in the tag line for a workout plan. She'd pay whatever they were charging.

"Now left."

She did it, but asked a breathy, "What?"

"Change directions." He pushed out a breath. "Makes you harder to hit."

Still, the gunshots kept coming. "Are they chasing us?"

He looked back. "I don't see them. But keep going. I'm not taking any chances."

They ran what was probably another half mile through the

wooded area around town. If they were even still close to it at all. Given how far they'd gone, Hollis had to believe they were miles from Last Chance. The open land, trees, and mountains—scary caves—stretched for nearly fifty miles. Hopefully they wouldn't have to walk a marathon or more just to get help.

She'd have a blister by then. Add that to her broken arm. At least she'd thrown up the contents of her stomach. Also, it kind of felt like she had a blister already, but to be fair, she had worse problems to worry about right now.

She hissed out a breath.

"We can slow down."

She held her right wrist against her stomach with her left hand.

"You okay?"

She glanced back, but saw only trees. No movement. Not even a scared animal racing away. "Now that I'm less occupied, my wrist hurts. A lot."

"Do you think it's broken?"

Hollis groaned. "I hope not. I have no idea what that's supposed to feel like. I've only ever broken my toes. Never any big bones."

"Really?" He walked alongside her. "Never?"

She shrugged. "Nope."

"Wow." He grinned, face flushed. Skin smeared with grit from the road, which she was absolutely *not* going to brush away with her good hand.

Maybe if this was Phil she'd have done it. But the lying, weasely FBI agent who'd *arrested* her didn't deserve even that much kindness. Never mind that he'd recently saved her from being shot.

"Why do you look mad now?"

Hollis glanced at the terrain in front of them. To the left, it angled up. The top was snowcapped since they were high enough in elevation to get those gorgeous white flakes in October. She was just glad it never snowed in town where she'd actually have to deal with them. The air was chilled, but that was fine with her because exertion and pain had left her sweating.

She thought over the contents of her purse and whether anything would actually be useful to get them out of this mess in one piece. Or if she even had the energy to dig around for something.

Will sighed. "Why do I feel bad that you're mad at me? Like I should apologize, or something."

"Maybe you should."

He was quiet for a moment. Then finally, he said, "Maybe we should just not talk about that. First priority is getting to a phone, or finding a ride out of here."

She could see that being a good idea. Better than arguing while they were out here, exposed. No food. No water.

She motioned to the southeast. "We should head in that direction."

It wasn't like there was a trail out here. Or any property boundary lines. This was all Bureau of Land Management acreage. Maybe they could find a ranger station. Get help by using a radio—and raid the snacks.

As if on cue, her stomach rumbled.

Will chuckled. "I second that." He rubbed his own abdomen, and she studied him out the corner of her eye until he said, "What?"

"You just...look different, I guess." She wasn't sure why she'd said that, or even how to explain. "I got used to Phil."

"Because you could control him. You knew where you stood, and that he'd do what you wanted."

"That was really who you wanted to be in the relationship? You could have chosen any persona, and that's what you chose?" Never mind that he thought she'd been all about Phil purely because she wanted someone she could manipulate. He'd played a part in all this as well.

He shrugged. "It served a purpose."

Gah. Why did he have to tie her up in knots? So what if he was right. She hadn't manipulated Phil, but he'd been a safe place where she didn't have to face anything she didn't want. Maybe too safe. She'd been content to leave, if only because she felt the need to start over somewhere no one could tie her up and drag her down.

Hollis was done drowning.

It was time to swim.

"Yeah." She lifted her chin and tried to sound cold, like she'd only been after what she wanted in the relationship. "I guess it did. And now it's done."

Let him think she didn't care. That she'd, in her own way, been using Phil as much as he'd been using her. She wasn't going to mull over whether or not that was true. It was done, so she might as well let it go. Focus on what was right in front of them instead.

Like the fire road they were coming up on.

Her shoe was beginning to seriously rub on the back of her right foot. Given how much her wrist hurt, it didn't factor too much on her list of priorities. But she was going to retitle the mental list. Instead of "Problems," she figured she could call it "Things Will Briar Did to Ruin My Life." Might not mean anything in the grand scheme of things, but it was pretty satisfying.

"There it goes again."

Hollis ignored his assessment of her mood. "You're the one who agreed we should leave it alone. So, don't bother bringing it up again. I think you've done enough already, considering we're lost in the middle of nowhere with no way to get back to Last Chance and armed men right behind us."

"I know." His tone was dark, but a whole lot softer than she'd have thought. "I could use a weapon to defend us right about now."

She stopped. That inventory she'd done of her purse.

Will swung around and faced her.

Hollis held one strap of her purse open with her good hand. "Inside zipper pocket."

He lifted one eyebrow. "What am I going to find?"

Scary girl things, no doubt. But also, something helpful. "Small canister."

He tugged it out with minimal rummaging. "Pepper spray?"

She grinned up at him. "Pepper spray."

"This is good. Thanks." He didn't break their locked gazes, just stayed there with his body close enough so she could feel the warmth of him even though they weren't touching. Finally, he said, "How is your arm?"

"Can you get that white bottle at the bottom?" She had drugstore pain meds. Even if they did nothing to cut down on the pain, she still wanted to give the full dose a try. Hollis winced. She'd have to swallow them without water.

He shook a few pills into her good hand.

She threw them back and gagged a couple of times, but managed to get them down. "Yuck." Hollis shuddered.

"We should keep going." And yet, he hadn't moved.

Hollis strode around him. She headed toward town, refusing to care how long this was going to take. Or that she should probably have also had him get a bandage from the little First Aid kit she had in the side pocket. But the irritation in the back of her foot was a good trick to remind her she shouldn't get comfortable. This man had arrested her.

He actually thought she was West. Which was *crazy*.

She might not have done everything right, and she might have people in her life who were prepared to do whatever they wanted—regardless of the legality of it—but that didn't mean she was like them.

Which was exactly why she'd been prepared to leave town. To get away from all the negative influences.

Until Frankie was kidnapped.

Hollis looked at the sky, fighting back tears. She'd just tell him it was about her wrist if he asked. Will didn't need to know.

He was a cop, and she wasn't supposed to tell any of them what was going on. She'd have to get that flash drive back from him—how, she had no idea. Then, she needed to charge her phone.

After that, she'd contact them and find out what she was supposed to do to get him back, now that everything had gone wrong.

And why hadn't she figured it would all fall apart? Everything else in her life did, so why not this too? Hollis scoffed aloud. She was such an idiot. *Of course* it would get messed up. The worst would happen.

It always did.

This was probably just some kind of cosmic justice directed at her for trying to leave and find a better life. If she believed the world worked like that, which she wasn't sure she did. Hollis had tried to fit in at the church. She'd even tried to join the choir, wearing her nicest clothes. That old church lady had taken one look at Hollis's knees and curled her lip. Then she'd commented, something about loose women.

Hollis hadn't gone back.

Her life was supposed to have gotten better, and it had not.

When Frankie had been kidnapped, she'd told only her mom. And then not only had Will been beaten, but her diner was set on fire, and she was arrested. Hollis didn't know if there was one perpetrator in all that, but if there was, she'd point her finger squarely at her mother.

Like always.

When her phone was charged, after she spoke with the kidnappers and figured this out, Hollis needed to have a serious chat with her mother.

The ground dipped to a stream in front of her. Probably shin deep, maybe to her knees. She'd bet it was ice-cold snow runoff. Just thinking about going in made her shudder, but Hollis didn't see a way across.

"Let me." Will moved around her. Mr. Special Agent

assessed the situation, walking down the bank, until he said, "We can cross here."

She went to see what he'd found. Several big boulders. "Those look slippery."

"Maybe so, but unless you want to add drenched to your list of ailments—as well as freezing and injured—these are our best bet."

"I don't gamble."

He lifted one eyebrow, but said nothing. "I'll go first, just in case."

Hollis just waited. If he wanted to play the hero, that was fine with her. When he tumbled over and was swept downstream, she would continue on without him. No point trying to find him when her time would be better served going for help and leaving his rescue to the professionals.

Keep telling yourself you don't care about him.

She didn't, so that was fine.

Will could go his way, and she would go hers. Though, if he arrested her again, that might be difficult. Maybe it was better to just ditch him somewhere. Get away, figure this out. She could talk to his FBI colleague afterwards and explain everything. Prove her innocence.

But she couldn't do that with Mr. Undercover here trying to take her in. Determined to believe what was on the flash drive was more than a fabrication—someone's attempt to implicate her.

She could keep herself safe. Especially if there was even a tiny chance Will had something to do with it. After all, she'd been given a flash drive of false evidence, and he just happened to find it? That was way too much of a coincidence.

She had to do this alone if she was going to stop the kidnappers from killing Frankie.

"Seems sturdy enough." He took another step. The boulder shifted. Will held his arms out to steady his balance. Waiting to see if he was going to fall, or if the boulder would hold.

Hollis cut right and ran along the bank, desperation fueling every step.

She had to get away from him.

"Hollis!"

She didn't stop. She just kept running.

10

Will shifted to go after her. His boot slipped on the boulder, and he overcorrected. He shifted his body upstream so he didn't wind up falling downstream and getting swept away. He hit the water and hissed as his knee and one hand landed in the freezing stream. Will had just enough wherewithal to keep the pepper spray can out of the water.

He didn't need to lose his only weapon.

The cold was a shock that eclipsed all thought, but he forced his mind to keep moving. *Hollis.* Thinking of her got him through it.

He scrambled up and got out of the water. Will's entire body shuddered, but he shook it off. It occurred to him he probably looked like a dog shaking off water. Why was he thinking of such nonsense right now?

Get moving.

He took off after her, boots squishing in the soft embankment beside the stream. She'd seriously ditched him. Will could hardly believe she'd waited until he got halfway across and then just raced away, leaving him alone in the middle of nowhere. Staying together was better. Even if they were at odds with each other.

Now she was so far ahead that he could barely make her out.

The woman was a fast runner, he had to admit that surprised him. Sure, she'd walked without complaint or tiredness so far. She ran for her workouts—she'd told Phil that. He pushed through all the fatigue and lingering aches and went after her. Annoyance and frustration fueled him, providing the energy he needed to try and run as faster than her.

Will had to face the fact then that he was probably just a bull-headed special agent. One who had misjudged this woman. Not that she'd proven to be more heinous than he thought. No, but she'd surprised him. Hollis had stuck with him. She'd run from bullets with him. She could have used that pepper spray on him, but she hadn't.

She'd given it to him instead. So that he had a weapon if he needed one.

But why give up her only weapon? Unless she knew she was in no danger.

The thought spurred him on. The men chasing the two of them? They might be trying to *rescue* her, not hurt her. She would get away. From him, as well as getting away from the consequences of her actions. Whatever they had been, she clearly saw a reason to ditch him and keep her secrets intact.

This fight to find West and bring her to the FBI was proving to be tougher than he'd expected. But then, since when had life ever gone to plan? Certainly never, not that he remembered at least. He should be better at rolling with the punches. And entirely more accustomed to being ditched by a woman—both literally and figuratively.

That was nothing new.

To be fair, he couldn't say he normally tried arresting the women he'd been interested in.

Conversation in lower octaves drifted to him, above the rhythmic heavy fall of his feet, and the sound of every exhale.

Two men appeared to his right, far enough away he could just make them out.

He stopped fast, using a downed tree and a copse of bushes for cover as he watched them make their way through the woods toward the stream. Had they seen Hollis? Maybe they were coming to meet her. That meant Will would simply be collateral damage, nothing to lose sleep over, even if he was an FBI agent.

Both men had guns out. Will watched them approach, assessing the situation as he tried to figure out what danger they posed. How to subdue them. How he should go about finding Hollis.

She would be long gone by the time he divested these two of their weapons. Or, if she really was trying to meet up with them, he would finally know the truth. And exactly what kind of person she was.

Will watched for her. Meanwhile, the two men came close enough so that he got a good look at their faces. They were the two guys from the diner. The ones who'd tied him to that chair and smacked him around before setting the diner on fire, trying to burn him to death in the process.

His whole body surged toward them, but Will caught himself before giving away his position. Armed with only pepper spray. While these two both held pistols.

"See her?" That, coming from the one who'd seemed to be in charge back in the diner office.

"Nah," his friend said. "Maybe it was a deer or something, I just thought it was her."

"You saw her. Which way was she going?"

The guy waved in the right direction. "Up there."

"That really narrows it down, genius." He looked like he wanted to slap his friend up the backside of his head. "Get up there and keep looking. Call me if you spot her."

"Fine." He huffed out a breath and trotted away, looking irritated. That left Will with the one he should get revenge on for nearly killing him—and all because he was a Fed. How they'd found that out might be worth asking. If he could question the guy while he pummeled him. Seemed like Hollis genuinely hadn't known, so he didn't think she'd sold him out. But someone had—and not knowing who it was would be even more dangerous.

But, first things first. He needed to get this guy subdued, get his gun and phone, and be creative about what to do with him. Will didn't want to walk the guy back to Last Chance tied up. It would take forever. And he didn't want kill the guy. But he couldn't just leave him walking around, either. The guy likely intended to harm good people.

Which meant Will could allow himself to get creative.

So this was going to be fun.

"I hear you."

Will didn't move.

"I hunted with my daddy every weekend, all season, every year of my whole life." The guy turned slowly. "You think I don't know when something's hiding. When I'm being watched."

Will held still until the guy's back was turned away from him. He launched up from his hiding spot and raced across the thirty or so feet that separated them.

The man spun, gun up.

Will bobbed and came up with his arm outstretched and sprayed the man in the face with the pepper spray. He cried out, and Will used the distraction and momentary blindness to grab for the gun. Will tackled the man to the ground.

They fell with a grunt. Will slammed his elbow into the man's nose while he rubbed at his eyes, trying to shove the big FBI agent off at the same time.

Will grabbed the gun and used it to break the guy's nose.

The guy clasped his face with both hands. Will stood, holding the gun on the man. "Don't move."

"What was that...pepper spray?" The guy tried to blink up at him.

"Don't rub your eyes. You need to rinse them."

The man called him a couple of choice words.

"That might be true, but you still didn't manage to kill me." Will held aim, part of his attention on the woods around him as he waited—and hoped—for the other guy to appear. Or Hollis. He'd have to deal with either. "So, who sent you?"

The man only cried out.

Will held the gun on him with one hand and used the other to flip the guy over. He fought the concept, but with pepper spray in his eyes and facing a rather large FBI agent, there wasn't much he could do.

The back pocket in his jeans held the man's wallet. Will pulled it out and flipped it open one handed to find an expired driver's license and a picture that matched the man in front of him. "Arnold Tenor."

A biker had been murdered a few months back. Will wondered if Karl Tenor was a relation of this guy.

"So, Arnie. Who do you work for, huh? Who wants the diner destroyed—and me dead?" When he said nothing, Will continued, "Probably someone looking to blame Hollis. Or cashing in on an insurance payment after an FBI agent is found dead inside."

Will moved down to the man's boots and pulled them off. He tossed them in the direction of the stream, but didn't manage to get them into the water. Then he pulled off the man's belt.

He didn't want the guy coming after him, and he had a decent amount of payback to dish out. Or wanted to, but probably shouldn't.

Will had to make sure this guy wasn't able to attack him before they reached Last Chance. But he also didn't want to be cruel. Nor did he want to tie the guy up so wolves, or a bear, could find him.

He winced, pocketed the guy's wallet, and stood.

Then he knocked Arnold out as cleanly as he could, without

lasting damage. He'd only be out a couple of minutes. Plenty of time for Will to use the belt to secure his hands together. The man would still have the use of his hands, but it would be awkward. More than the concessions they'd given him when they tried to kill him.

But this was proving to everyone that Will was the better man. After which he would find Hollis and sort this mess out.

Will took his phone and used the man's thumbprint to unlock it, before taking a few snaps of the man's face and a few that clearly identified the location of where Arnold could be found. Will disabled the thumb print ID feature straight away, then made sure no one was about to sneak up on him as he made a call.

"Chief Barnes, Last Chance Police Department." This was his cell number, but probably the number wasn't labeled in Conroy's contacts.

"It's Will."

Silence. "Who?"

"FBI Special Agent Will Briar. I left with Hollis?" He explained to the very quiet police chief what had happened.

Conroy's end of the line rustled. "We're on our way. Stay on this line, and I'll have Ted trace the call. We'll find you."

"Okay, cause I'm looking for Hollis and the other guy. She's got a broken arm so medical supplies would be good."

"Copy that." He heard Conroy relay the information to whoever was with him. "It'll be thirty minutes."

"I'm putting the phone in my pocket, but I'll leave the line open. I need both hands."

"Copy."

Will stuffed the phone in his back pocket. He raced in the direction the other man had gone, Arnold Tenor's friend.

He had to find her. She was either getting away, or that man was here to hurt her. Will didn't want what had happened to him to happen to anyone else. Least of all Hollis.

A scream up ahead spurned him on. Will held the gun up

and ran flat out. He was tempted to pray, which he always did when he needed that little bit of extra help. He'd just never admitted that to anyone. No one should know he sometimes thought he might not be able to succeed.

Especially when so much was on the line.

He wanted to get out of Last Chance. Which meant this case had to be over.

There. "Hey!"

The man spun, and Will realized he'd shouted aloud. He lifted his gun. Will lifted his. Shots rang out.

Will dove to the ground, which didn't feel super good. His feet were almost numb. Everything was stiff, and his hip hurt like crazy from hitting that rock. He rolled over and stopped with his stomach to the ground and both arms stretched out in front of him, finger on the trigger. He fired again.

The shot went wide.

Will heard a whimper, and everything in him stilled. The man hauled Hollis in front of him and turned his gun so it pointed at the side of her neck.

"You want me to kill her, that's on you."

Will moved his finger from the trigger.

Hollis's gaze flew around, and then she found him. A cry escaped her lips. "Will."

It was the sweetest, most awful sound in the world.

Will stood. "Don't hurt her. Just let her go, and you can go on your way. No harm. No foul. Go find Arnold and get out of here."

The old "live to fight another day" tactic was appreciated by a lot of bad guys who knew the cost of the rough lives they lived. Would this one take that olive branch?

The man backed up a step, dragging Hollis with him.

"No way." The man bit out, "She comes with me."

11

"No." She didn't want to go with him. And as much as she'd wanted to leave Will behind—and in the past—right now Hollis would prefer to be with him than with this guy, or alone. "I'm not going with you."

"Then I'll shoot you right now," he said to her in a low voice. "And she don't get paid."

She? The only "she" Hollis could think he might be talking about was her mother. The one to whom she'd gone for help when she was told Frankie had been kidnapped. *She don't get paid.* She hoped that didn't mean what it sounded like.

There was no time right now to figure it out.

"Will."

He said, "Let her go." His expression deadly serious.

"Don't test me. I'm the one with the power here," the guy holding onto her said. "So put your gun on the ground. Yeah, put it down."

Was he making this up as he went along? That was never good. She didn't want to die. At least not while Frankie was still a kidnap victim. "Don't do this."

Will's mouth shifted. She could see he wanted to do something. But he also felt powerless—she could see it in his eyes. In that moment, despite what was happening to her, she also wanted to help him. Even though he'd arrested her. Even though he'd treated her like a low-life suspect.

Hollis hadn't seen the documents on the flash drive, but even she knew "criminal conspiracy" couldn't be good.

Even so, she'd fallen for Phil. But, she also had to concede, at least in part, that she'd fallen for Will. He might argue otherwise, since Phil had been an undercover alias. But there had to be at least a tiny measure of himself in the persona of the man she'd started dating.

The man she'd been prepared to leave.

Hollis wanted to sigh over how complicated her life was right now, but the man holding her squeezed her arm. He jerked her closer to him, and the gun dug into the skin of her neck. "I said put your gun down!"

"You know I'm FBI. We don't do that."

Hollis blinked. He was just going to let this guy shoot her? She opened her mouth to beg him to do something when Will lifted his gun up and to the right. He fired off a single shot past the gunman's shoulder.

She flinched anyway. She let out a squeal and tried to duck away from it.

The gunman moved his weapon away from her to fire at Will. Hollis wrenched herself from his grip as he took aim on the Fed. She stumbled and went down. A gun went off.

Hollis threw her arms over her head and just stayed down. If Will was dead, and that guy was going to kill her or take her like they'd taken Frankie, she didn't even want to know. Hollis would rather not see it coming.

"Hey." A gentle hand touched her shoulder.

Hollis flinched and looked over her shoulder but didn't lower her arms. Will gathered her to him. She was crouched, so she basically just lost her balance and fell into him. Her arms still up. So when he wrapped his arms around her waist, hers lowered to settle on his shoulders. A strong hug. The place of safety she'd first felt with Phil.

But now she felt so much more.

This man was strong where Phil had been malleable. He'd stepped up for her. Put his life on the line.

She'd saved him from that fire and, yes, he'd arrested her. But, he'd been there when their car was run off the road. And now, he'd killed a man for her.

Or so she presumed. Hollis was *not* going to take a look.

She sighed and his arms tightened around her in a way that was more comforting than anything she'd ever felt before. "What are we going to do?"

Their relationship, if it could be called that, was so mixed up. There was probably no way to unravel it. If he even wanted to help her try. Maybe he still just wanted to take her in to the FBI office for questioning. All so he could close this case.

Will shifted, and he pulled back. He seemed to realize she was in his arms and got all stiff as he stood. "We should get going. There's no point waiting out here when it's going to get dark soon."

He turned away, leaving her to clamber to her feet without assistance. Hollis had to get up one handed. The other one was all swollen now. It did not feel good, and when she rose to her feet, she swayed. Woozy. Will caught her elbow. But he didn't hug her again.

"I'm okay."

Will gave her elbow a squeeze and let go like she'd burned his hand.

Of course, she was absolutely *not* okay, and they both knew it. But that was hardly the point since nothing had been resolved between them.

Apparently, it wasn't going to be. Will would continue to treat her like a criminal, and Hollis would have to figure out how to save Frankie before everything got worse.

"Hollis!" That was Mia.

"Will!" And Conroy.

They were accompanied by two other officers, both wearing SWAT-type gear. No helmets, though. Just boots and padding, gloves—like they were planning on maybe going rock climbing.

Mia ran straight to her and enveloped her in a hug, but, in doing so, clipped Hollis's wrist. She tried to hold back a scream.

"Oh no." The Lieutenant's voice was slightly louder than it needed to be. Mia was still awaiting a surgery that would hopefully give her a considerable amount of her hearing back. Until then, she was confined to doing paperwork at the office. And doing the lunch run to pick up everyone's sandwiches from the diner. Lately, at least. Apparently, right now, she was field certified.

"It's fine." Hollis made sure her lips moved clearly, so Mia would be able to read them. She lifted her arm and showed Mia. "I think I broke it."

Mia slid her arm along Hollis's shoulder and turned them both towards the men. "My friend needs medical attention." She practically shouted.

They had her sit on an overturned log which probably housed a million bugs underneath. Thinking about them, even though they hadn't crossed her mind this entire time until just now, was better than how it felt to have her wrist wrapped. Even when the officer handed her an ice pack to put on it. The bizarre mental reprieve was nice.

"Long day, huh?"

The nameplate on his shirt said, BASUTO. He'd responded to the diner fire, and his mother was in the church choir Hollis had tried to join. Mama Basuto was one of the nice, older women at church.

Hollis registered what he'd said and glanced at Will. "I have this feeling it's not over yet."

Basuto chuckled. A low rumble that sounded nice.

But Hollis couldn't relax. And she certainly wasn't in the place to be soothed. They still had to walk out of here.

Basuto squeezed her shoulder. "Stuart and Dean are on their way with a couple of ATVs, so you'll be able to get a ride back to town."

"Did you guys walk?"

"More like ran." Basuto motioned at Conroy, who was standing beside Will but ignoring the Fed's attempts to talk to him. "The chief wanted to get here as quickly as possible."

Conroy nodded, as though to confirm.

Will said, "Someone should go find this guy's partner. They're the ones who burned down the diner and attacked me."

"They are?"

Everyone glanced at her at the same time. Hollis felt the prickle of so much attention all at once on the back of her neck. She glanced down and adjusted the cold pack on her arm.

"I'll go." Basuto said, "Soon as Dean and Stuart get here, I'll pull some supplies together and head out."

"Sounds good to me."

Hollis hadn't been expecting to face Stuart, though she'd spoken with his wife, Kaylee, already today. Why not? After all, she was only supposed to be long gone from town by now.

Instead, she was injured and a whole group of people had come to rescue them.

My friend needs medical attention.

Hollis had never counted Mia a friend. Then again, she didn't especially count anyone in town as a friend. She had a whole lot of acquaintances and saw many of them every day as they came in and out of the diner. But at the end of her shift, she left alone, and then went home to her apartment. To be alone.

The last thing she'd ever wanted to do was make a plan to be sociable with even more people after a long day at work.

Until Phil.

But that had hardly been real, had it? Now she knew it was a lie. And the people she'd never considered friends before were now claiming her as one. What would her mom have said if she'd heard Mia's words? Aside from laughing, she'd probably think nothing of it. Her mom didn't care enough to have an opinion on anything to do with Hollis. Except being jealous of her jacket.

Why was today proving to be so confusing?

It didn't make sense when her life had always been rather dull.

Will and Conroy had wandered over to the man's body. She saw the gunshot wound in the middle of the red stain on the front of the man's shirt. It wasn't long before Conroy came back to Hollis, still standing beside Mia. "Are you up for a question or two before your ride gets here?"

"That's fine." She shrugged one shoulder.

"You mentioned Frankie right before you left the police station. Why?"

You call the police… "I was just…worried. The diner and all. You know?"

Conroy's expression shifted, just a tiny bit. Like when it was obvious someone didn't like their meal, but they were trying to be nice about it.

"Why do you ask?"

"I just wanted to know if there was a problem I should look into." Conroy slid his arm around Mia's shoulders and tugged her to his side. Their wedding was scheduled for just a few weeks from now. Hollis hadn't planned to be there. Now she almost wished she was going to stick around long enough to see what everyone had been waiting for all these months.

Before Hollis could say anything, he continued, "After you left, I called Frankie, but he didn't pick up. The unit I sent to his house said no one was there, so I called your mom. She told me he was with her. She even put him on the phone."

"What? You *talked* to him?"

"Yeah." Conroy shook his head. "Why?"

"What's going on, Hollis?"

She ignored Will's question. "This is crazy. They called me and said he was kidnapped."

Everyone started talking at once. Apparently, withheld information was a big deal to cops. Plus it seemed they were freaking out about Frankie being kidnapped, as though it had just happened. Finally, Conroy lifted his hand and commanded silence.

"One at a time."

Basuto said, "*Kidnapped.*"

Mia glanced around, reading lips. Will turned to Hollis, "Why didn't you tell me? I'd have helped you, but you said nothing."

"They told me not to tell the cops, or they'd kill him. I didn't know it at the time, but it turns out *you're the cops.*" She looked at Conroy. "He's really fine?"

Conroy nodded.

"This makes no sense." What on earth was going on? "He's with *her*. Even *that* should mean he's not fine. But he is."

Her dad—stepdad. Her mom.

Together?

Hollis, caught in the middle again. Plus, gunmen chasing them. The chief and his fiancé were here. Basuto, too. And now that the others were on their way to help, she could see that an entire team was rallying to provide aid, and not just because Will was involved.

No, they'd come here to help. Her.

Hollis couldn't even begin to figure all this out.

Now, more than ever before, she really did need to leave town and start over somewhere else. A place where things would actually make sense for once.

12

Conroy hung up the phone. "Eric is on his way."

"Great." Will clenched his molars. It wasn't worth trying to smile. "How long until he gets here?"

That would give him a timeline on how long he had to solve this case. If he could hand Special Agent Cullings the full explanation when he walked in the door…Will could imagine the satisfaction. The look on his handler's face when he realized Will had figured it all out.

Conroy looked at his watch. "Four hours, probably. Even with the FBI chartering a plane."

Good. That had to be enough time. Will stood, "I'm going to go talk to the guy we brought in."

The cops had rounded up the man Will had subdued. He was here now, and Will needed answers from him. Hollis was at the hospital getting her wrist looked at. Then she'd be brought back here.

"Let's check with Ted first." Conroy met Will at the door to his office. "See if he got anything from the guy's phone." But he didn't exit the office. He said, "You don't want to wait, debrief with Eric, and figure this all out together?"

"No point sitting around until he gets here." Will shrugged. "Not when we can get the ball rolling and maybe get answers."

Conroy nodded. "Fair enough."

He led the way through the office to the back hall. Will spotted Savannah, the police detective, and Mia at their desks. He lifted his chin to them. These people had come and rescued him and Hollis. They'd brought their guns and driven miles into the middle of nowhere to bring the two of them back and get this case put to bed.

He owed them.

Will figured solving this case, and finally finding West after they'd all been trying to identify him—or her—for months now, would be good payback. He really had thought it might be Hollis. After all, it was clear he could be swayed by his feelings.

No more, though.

Now he knew her stepfather had been abducted, it made a lot more sense that she'd acted strangely. But it still didn't answer all of his questions.

Conroy knocked on the door frame of Ted's office. The department's technical specialist was in a relationship with Officer Jess Ridgeman, granddaughter of the previous chief. This police department had a seriously high ratio of officers involved with each other. It made Will wonder if there was something in the water. Maybe they were all drinking out of the same fountain and it was contaminated.

He didn't envy Conroy the job of making sure no one's personal bias got in the way of police work—especially his own.

Once this case was done, Will would be out of here. It had been years since he worked from the FBI office he was technically assigned to. Maybe he'd ask for a transfer. Start over somewhere new. Or leave the FBI and take a different job. Go into the private sector in some fashion.

Ted spotted them in the doorway. He started, then pulled the air pod from his left ear. "Hey."

Will said, "Anything on the phone?"

Conroy glanced at Will. Ted nodded, typing on his computer faster than Will would ever be able to, even if he practiced every day for the rest of his life. "Do you want the results of the contents of the flash drive first?"

"The one I found on Hollis?"

"Yes." Ted continued, "I had a look at the oh-so-incriminating evidence. It's all fake."

"Are you *serious*?"

Ted glanced over at him. "And Arnold Tenor's call history indicates he called one number more than anyone else."

"Girlfriend?" Conroy asked.

"If it is," Ted said, "he's having a thing with Hollis's mom."

Will had seen Sharleen. She might be attractive, but the hard way she lived had given her a brittleness that was not cute. Her personality was equally as abrasive. Hollis, on the other hand, was soft. In every way, including the one that took up far too much of his attention.

Will ran his hands down his face. Hollis was innocent, but her mother was the one mixed up in the middle of this? Her diner had been targeted. Her stepfather had been kidnapped, and was now with the mother?

He should be thinking about Sharleen right now, but instead his thoughts inevitably strayed to Hollis.

Was her arm broken? He wanted to call and find out, but her phone was dead, and he didn't even know where his was. Shattered. An officer had been dispatched to the accident site to secure the scene and wait for the tow truck. They had orders to grab all his stuff out of the trunk.

Until he had that, he only had his wallet and badge. Nothing else.

Why did he want to be at the hospital sitting with her, waiting to find out the extent of her injuries? He should be glad he was here so he could wrap all this up. She would at least be safe. Will no longer thought Hollis was the main suspect, but if her mother was involved, he still needed to entertain an aiding and abetting charge. So then, maybe she *would* find herself in jail.

The clock was ticking.

Here, he was useless. He couldn't stop thinking about Hollis, as though his heart was attuned to her. And his brain followed his heart, down that rabbit hole. When he returned back to reality, he realized he hadn't gotten anything done.

Will had been dealing with these same daydreams, ever since he realized she might be involved in the case, and he'd told Eric he planned to get close to her and find out for sure. Eric hadn't thought anything of it. Will had never fallen for a suspect before.

That wasn't going to happen now. He couldn't let it. If he was with her now, he'd be asking about her mom's romantic life. Questioning her. He wasn't going to say interrogate.

"Let's go talk to him." Will backed up a step and pivoted on the ball of his foot. He assumed Conroy was going to follow. He just wanted to get this done instead of being continually distracted by thoughts of Hollis.

The pain in her eyes. The sheen of tears. The way she'd ditched him. His hip still hurt, but his clothes were dry now, at least. Two cups of coffee, and he was good.

Ten minutes later, they had the suspect in the interview room. Conroy had sent an officer to check on Sharleen and Frankie and ask some questions. He'd also had Ted print him out a copy of the call history and texts from the phone. Will pulled out a chair and sat without wincing, even though the bruise on his hip was still fresh. Conroy set the pages down beside Will and remained standing.

"We meet again." Will folded his arms. "Arnold Tenor."

The man who'd beaten him and tried to burn him alive— the one Will had left in the middle of nowhere tied up—sniffed and glared at him. He wore a gray jumpsuit now. Hair mussed.

"You look like you could use some coffee." Will motioned over his shoulder with his thumb. "Wanna cup?"

"Not unless you pour something stronger in it."

"Ah." Will nodded. "I'd need a drink too, if I was stringing along a woman like Sharleen. I'd probably have a stomach ulcer."

The skin around Arnold's eyes contracted.

"But maybe she's nice to you. Or maybe she's mean, and you like your relationships like that."

Arnold made a face. "It ain't like that."

"No? Then tell me. What's it like? Because the last time I saw you, I was about to be burned alive."

"Cause you're a *Fed*."

"I know," Will said, "on account of you sitting on that side of the table, while I get to sit on this side. With the Last Chance chief of police."

Arnold curled his lip.

"So, who told you to burn down the diner?"

Arnold sneered. "West."

Will chuckled. "That sounds familiar. So far it's been a pretty good line, keeping the cops chasing after someone who's turning out to be nothing but a ghost." Let this guy think Will didn't even believe West existed. "Probably just a made-up story. No one's looking for a real person, am I right?"

"Sure. West doesn't exist." Arnold nodded. "That sounds right."

Will figured Arnold was planning to just string him along, to see how this all worked out. The guy had one card to play, and that was the information he knew.

Will said, "Tell me what West has to do with you and Sharleen."

"What makes you think I have anything to do with Sharleen?"

Will tapped his index finger on the papers. "This. Your phone records. So, is it business, or pleasure, this thing you've got going on with her?"

"It can't be both?"

"What were you and your friend looking for in the diner office?"

"Stuff."

"Wow, this is such a productive conversation. I can't believe how much information you're bombarding me with. I can hardly handle it."

Arnold smirked.

"Who is West?"

Arnold pressed his lips together.

"You know. So tell me."

"And if I tell you, what do I get then?" Arnold directed his question to Conroy, then glanced at Will.

Conroy said, "Depends on what you want."

"Between the police department here in Last Chance, and the FBI, I'm sure we can come up with something." Will shrugged like it was no big deal. Not like the whole case was riding on what this man had to tell them. "We'll see what we can do."

"Not good enough." Arnold shook his head. "If I tell you what I know, I want a guarantee of a lesser charge. Something in writing with the DA's signature on it. Or the US Attorney. Whoever tells you guys what to do. I want something from *them*."

Will tried not to look as irritated as he was.

"Someone with more clout than y'all."

He stood, gathered up the papers, and walked to the door. When Conroy joined him in the hall and had shut the door, Will said, "That was a waste of time."

"Maybe." Conroy shrugged.

"I need to talk to Hollis. See what she knows."

"You still think she's deeply involved in all this?"

Will said, "I think she can wear a wire and go talk to her mom."

"I would never do that."

He spun and saw her at the end of the hall. Bandaged arm

in a sling. Pale face, probably too pale. She looked like she needed to sit down and eat a sandwich. Which, now that he was thinking about it, sounded really good.

Before he could say anything, she turned around and walked down the hall. Back to the main police station office.

Will sighed.

Conroy was shaking his head.

"What?"

The police chief grinned and slapped Will on the shoulder. "Good luck with that."

He left Will in the hallway wondering what that was about. Until he gave up trying to figure out Hollis and headed after her. She was over by the front desk, talking with Kaylee. The receptionist needed to let her sit down.

In fact...

Will dragged over a chair for her to be close to her friend. "Sit down."

Hollis lifted her eyebrows. "Thank you?"

"You're welcome." He strode to Conroy's office, but the man was on the phone. So Will detoured to Basuto's desk. The sergeant was working on his computer but looked up when Will got near. "Anything I should know?"

"Conroy is calling the DA to see if there's a possibility of a deal with a guy that has Arnold Tenor's record."

Will nodded. "Okay, thanks."

"There are a few left over sub sandwiches in the fridge if you want one."

He nodded again and helped himself, wondering if he should ask Hollis what she wanted. What he *should* be doing was asking her questions while she was off guard. Using her physical and mental state against her and getting her to let her guard down.

The way he'd done when he hugged her. That sweet moment in the middle of all this.

"Special Agent Briar!"

Will walked out of the kitchen chewing a huge bite of meatball sub. He lifted his chin at Basuto. Conroy was across the room at the door of his office.

The sergeant said, "Our officer who went to check on Frankie and Sharleen just radioed in." Hollis started to object. Before she could say anything, Basuto continued, "Front door was open. They're both gone, and there are signs of a struggle."

13

Hollis sank into her chair. She reached for her phone, but it wasn't done charging. She powered it up anyway.

Frankie *had* been kidnapped. But now it turned out he wasn't *actually* kidnapped. He was fine. He was with her mother—whatever that was all about.

Now they were both missing. *Signs of a struggle.*

"This makes no sense."

Mia came over, leaning against the desk opposite her. Relaxed. Calm and in control. "We'll find them. I know telling you not to worry is going to be futile, but you really don't need to worry."

Hollis nodded. The phone loaded. She navigated to the photo she'd been sent, the one of a bloody and gagged Frankie.

She held it up with her good hand so they could see the screen. "He was kidnapped."

Mia said, "No one thought you were lying." She paused. "Did you think that we did?"

Hollis didn't need a therapist right now. "I'm actually not as confused that Frankie had being abducted, as I am about the fact he was fine this whole time, and with *her*."

"Is there somewhere you can think of they might have gone

together? A place they might hide out, if someone was looking for them?"

She shook her head, but tried to think it through while everyone in the room stared at her. Even Will. Why did he have to pin her with that rough-handsome stare? Especially now she knew it was all about him being a Special Agent, his focus on her solely because she was a suspected criminal.

He might know now that she wasn't West, but that didn't let her off the hook as far as he was concerned. She'd thought on it while they were X-raying her arm and wrapping it in the temporary cast they'd given her to wear until the swelling went down and they could put the real cast on for a few weeks. All Hollis's mind lingered on was the diner. But how did West link to it?

And what did all this have to do with that flash drive of fake incriminating evidence?

Someone had wanted her to be implicated as West. She'd always figured the notorious West and connected criminal activity was actually the work of a few people. Or maybe like a ghost he only operated in the shadows, and would never be identified. Given more than one founder of Last Chance had been exposed over wrongdoing lately, she'd figured it was one of them.

All she wanted to know was why she was being targeted. Considered expendable by someone, the mysterious "they" were trying to force the cops' hand. To put her in jail as West, so she'd take the fall for everything.

"Hollis."

She shook her head. "I don't think they've been in the same room as each other for…years. They got divorced when I was nine. They hate each other."

Her mom had tried to involve Frankie in some dirty business. He'd always grumbled about her voicemails, or how she'd send guys to lean on him about one deal or another. If there was someone laundering money through the diner, it was more likely to be her than Hollis. But how would her own mother set her up to take the fall as West?

Hollis didn't believe her mom was the person everyone knew as West. Sharleen was too selfish for that. She followed every whim, so long as it was in her best interest. West was far too coordinated. The whole operation had multiple moving parts, which spanned over the course of several months—the wheelhouse of countless different illegal activities.

Criminal conspiracy was a stretch for her mother, a woman who only thought about herself.

Mia said, "What are you thinking?"

Hollis shook her head again.

"We can't help you if you don't talk to us. The FBI is looking at you and any information you can give us only strengthens your case."

"I shouldn't have to prove my innocence."

Savannah moved in beside Mia. "Sometimes it's necessary."

When had the detective arrived? Wilcox was married to Tate Hudson. They'd eloped a few weeks back, and then disappeared on their honeymoon for a while.

Conroy rounded the desk to stand by his fiancé. "We want to help you." He motioned at the two women. "None of us want to see you convicted of something you didn't do."

"And if I did do it?" Wasn't like they'd stuck up for her earlier. They'd allowed Will to walk her out.

"You didn't. Ted already proved that everything found on the flash drive was a fabrication. The FBI has no grounds to accuse you of anything."

Will completed their huddle. "He's right. I'm sorry I arrested you, especially considering the fact that something is going on with Sharleen and Frankie."

That meant it would still have something to do with her. "I should've just left."

Conroy frowned. "What do you mean?"

Hollis sighed. "When I got that text—" She motioned to the

image on the phone. "—I was on my way out the door for an interview. I had my suitcase already packed. I wasn't planning on coming back to town. Ever."

Across the room, Kaylee gasped. The rest of them looked surprised, though no one was audible about it. Will looked mad. "You were leaving?"

She wanted to shrug off the question but couldn't quite do it. "The landlord for the diner can work with Frankie on where it goes next."

"And you're done? Just like that?" Kaylee strode over. "You weren't going to tell us, were you?"

Why would she have? It wasn't like they were...

"We're your friends!"

"Kaylee—"

"No." The receptionist shook her head. "I can't believe this. *Stuart* isn't going to believe this. You were just gonna walk out and leave them all in the lurch, not caring what happened next."

"I don't own the diner. I'm not the manager."

Kaylee made a pfft sound. "You run the place. Who else does all the work?"

"That was just because of Frankie's accident. He needs a push to get back to it." Truth was, she'd been worried about him lately. He was withdrawing in a way she didn't like. Becoming even more distant than before. "Now I'm wondering if he's been busy with *criminal conspiracy.*"

Will said, "Do you think he might be working something with Sharleen?"

"I don't know." She didn't know if she was supposed to care, or if it was better that she didn't. "How would I know? I barely speak to her, and I only talk to Frankie about one subject. The diner. Why would they even drag me into something like this?"

As far as she could see, they were free to do whatever they wanted with their lives. Preferably without dragging her into the middle of it. Why frame her, manipulating things so that she implicated herself, just to rescue Frankie from a fake kidnapping? The whole thing was seriously messed up.

Will asked Conroy a question, and the "cops" all got into a debate she didn't understand. Stuff about probable cause, and forensics. She'd seen enough cop shows on TV she could follow along, but this was her life. Somehow it just didn't seem as easy.

Her "parents" were nothing like the kind of people who were supposed to fill those roles in her life. They never had been, so she normally didn't miss it. She'd found it hard to miss what she hadn't ever had. But once in a while—like now—Hollis felt the sting. Especially when she was surrounded by good people who knew. People with compassion.

Knowing they saw people like her every day made it worse. That they worked to help them, and yet no one noticed Hollis.

Or, at her lowest, that was how it seemed to her.

She'd long given up wishing she could be on their side of things. People with loving relationships in their lives, and the resources to help others. The side that meant a good home life. A hot meal every night. A mom who wasn't intent on living a life of crime. But that wasn't the way her life had gone.

"Hollis?"

She looked at Mia. "Yes?"

"Do you think your mom would pick up if you called?"

"I have no idea. It's not guaranteed." Sometimes her mom didn't call back for two weeks—if she called back at all.

Mia glance at Conroy. "What about the flash drive, or gathering evidence at the diner or from Sharleen's place?"

Savannah said, "I can go canvas for witnesses, help with evidence collection."

"Do it." Conroy nodded.

Will scrubbed his hands down his face, then groaned. He rolled his shoulders.

Conroy said, "That's what happens when you jump the gun, arrest the wrong person, and wind up a target."

"Wow." Will blinked. "You're not even going to sugarcoat it?"

"Do I need to?"

"No."

"You don't work for me. Eric is the one I liaise with at the FBI. Not you."

Will's jaw flexed.

Hollis unplugged her phone, gathered her purse and stood. "I can go, right?" Her car was parked outside. She could head to her apartment for her suitcase and get going. No point in staying now, right? She was only delaying the fresh start she desperately needed by sticking around here just out of curiosity.

If she was the target of a frame job, there was even less reason to stick around Last Chance. She'd rather be as far from here as possible.

In a few weeks, when they'd figured it all out, she would read all about it in an online news article. Then she would forget everything about Last Chance.

Or anyone she might have felt an obligation towards. If Frankie was tied up with Sharleen, he didn't need her help anymore.

Hollis dug her keys out.

"Headed home?" Will moved close, speaking low, probably so no one else heard. "Rest sounds good." He lifted his brows and stretched again.

Hollis didn't need to be reminded she was attracted to him. "I figure if I leave in an hour, I can get somewhere with a hotel by tonight." She looked at the time on her phone.

"Wait. You're leaving as in *leaving*?"

Hollis just shrugged a little, not really sure what else to say. "I missed my interview, but maybe they'll understand, and allow me to reschedule it for tomorrow."

For the chance to manage her own restaurant, she would make it work.

"You're a target. Your life is in danger, which means the only place you're going is somewhere in protective custody." Before she could interrupt, he continued, "Even if that protective custody is your house, fine. But we need to make sure you're safe."

"I'm going." None of them had the right to keep her here against her will. Did they? "I'm not a suspect, I'm not a cop, and I don't want to be a part of this."

Will folded his arms. "Whether you want to or not, you still are."

"No, I'm not. Find West," she said. "Or not. I really don't care."

"And if Sharleen and Frankie get killed?"

"I'll come back for the funerals." She lifted her chin. "Maybe."

"You're better than that."

"You know what?" She took a step away from them. "You guys might think I am, but the truth is that I'm really not. They raised me. Not a loving parent, or people who follow the law."

"I wouldn't know. I had a gunnery sergeant for a father." Will said, "I'm pretty sure the back of my skull is flat, given how many times he slapped me upside the head."

"Why would that make me think twice about leaving?"

"The people who were supposed to teach us loving sacrifice, and how to be a functional law-abiding citizen often find that whole thing real difficult. Mostly because they have no clue how to do it themselves. They're still trying to figure it out."

"Sharleen was never trying."

"And yet you managed to know what doing the right thing is. In a way it's engrained in you."

"Usually it was whatever she *wasn't* doing." Which made her point now, didn't it? "Which means if she thinks sticking around Last Chance is the right thing, what I should do is leave."

"Someone needs to watch your back."

Hollis spun around to Conroy. "Do I have to stay?"

"This is an FBI case." The look on the police chief's face

gave away nothing. "If they think you should be in protective custody, it's on their dime."

It was like he wanted her to stay somewhere with the very Fed who'd arrested her. Hollis wanted to scream at him, ask him what he was even thinking. Instead, she took a deep breath and let it out slowly.

Before she could reason with them, Will said, "Doesn't matter where you're going, I'm your shadow until I know for sure you're not in danger."

14

"I know you don't want to be here." Will put the car in park. "This won't take long."

Hollis didn't reach for the door handle. She also didn't say anything.

"Okay?"

She shrugged one shoulder.

Will turned the car engine off. "How is your arm?"

"Fine." She stared out the window at her mom's townhome.

How was he supposed to admit to her that he needed her to help him figure out who West was? Especially after he'd accused *her* of committing the crimes. They'd been through plenty in the last 24 hours. She should be resting—not leaving town as planned. He was glad he'd insisted she come here with him instead.

"This really will only take a minute," he said. "I'd like you to just take a look inside. There are things you may notice that the techs going over the scene may not see as significant. Because they don't know…your mom."

"My mom, the victim?" she said. "Or my mom, the criminal who sent those two men to kill us?"

"Or…capture us," Will added. Then again, they'd been

forced off the road. So, she was probably right. "My boss will be here soon, and I want to have more for him than what I've got so far. Something concrete that can be quantified."

All this time and effort. They'd made several arrests and taken out a lot of bad people who had called Last Chance their home. Still, he hadn't finished this job. Will needed to identify West so he could finally label this case, "Closed."

"Great." She grasped the handle.

Will had to hustle around the car to meet her before she shut the door. Despite the word she'd chosen, he didn't believe she thought everything was great. In fact, she didn't look like she wanted to be anywhere near here.

He touched her shoulder. When she lifted her gaze the inch or so that separated their heights, he said, "Thank you."

She made a face, one that looked a whole lot like, "Whatever."

He gave her shoulder a small squeeze. "I still appreciate it."

They spoke with the uniformed officer Conroy had posted at the door. Inside, an officer on evidence collection was packing up. The guy lifted his chin, but said nothing.

Hollis stopped in the entryway. "What am I looking for?"

"Anything that might speak to what your mom has been up to."

Hollis turned to him. "And I'm just supposed to be impressed by your dedication to upholding the law? This isn't about me being where you are so you can do your FBI thing and protect me at the same time?"

Will heard a snort he was pretty sure came from the cop collecting evidence. "I just want to look around here. Then I think we both need a break and some food."

"I feel like I could sleep for a whole day, but my arm hurts so badly it would probably be impossible. I'd wind up tossing and turning trying to get comfortable."

Will gave her a conciliatory smile. He wanted to kiss her forehead, or hug her. Something. It was like a compulsion. He was attracted to her—seriously attracted to her. It wasn't just Phil who'd been invested in the relationship. And now that he knew she wasn't part of the criminal conspiracy case he was putting together? It was like the brake pedal had lifted.

"Last time I was here, I slapped a glass out of my mom's hand so hard it shattered across the kitchen."

"You guys fought?"

"She didn't care that Frankie had been kidnapped. I guess I know why now."

Will started to speak.

Hollis turned to the stairs. "Let's just get this over with."

She trudged up, Will following behind her, trying to figure out why she'd suddenly clammed up. What had he said or done? At the top of the stairs, she swayed slightly. Will touched her elbow. "We should go. You're not okay."

Hollis pulled her elbow from his hold. "I don't need to be babied. If I didn't think it would help, I wouldn't be here."

Will bit back what he wanted to say. Hollis continued on, and he followed like a lost puppy looking for scraps. "I'm not trying to baby you."

"Well then back off."

Will sighed.

She turned around, but before she could say whatever was on the tip of her tongue, Will said, "I had surgery."

Hollis frowned.

"About a year ago, on my shoulder." He'd never told anyone this story. "Soon as I was back at home, I figured I was all right. Enough I could ignore all the advice about having someone stay with you. I was gonna take a shower and planned to somehow put a new bandage on afterwards. So, I peeled off the bandage to get a look at the stitches, the wound, and I passed out. Hit my head on the bathtub and woke up with a concussion. All because I didn't want to admit I needed help."

Hollis's eyebrow rose.

"I don't think that's what you're doing. But I'm hypersensitive to the insistence of the injured trying to go at it alone."

Her expression softened. "It must have been awful, waking up in pain and not knowing what happened."

"It was." Will said, "I know what it feels like to be alone and scared."

Hollis closed the space between them and slid her good arm around his waist. Will laid his cheek against her hair. She said, "Sorry I'm not being very nice."

"Sorry I made you walk upstairs."

Her body shifted as she chuckled. "Being here is weird." She pulled back. "I don't think I've ever been upstairs in my mom's house. I don't even know which of these rooms is the bedroom, or the bathroom, or what?"

She wandered to the first door. As though they hadn't just had a sweet moment that warmed him more than any other experience of his life. Well, it was in the same ballpark as the other sweet moments the two of them had shared since their first meeting.

He followed her into a room. Still feeling like a puppy, just not quite so lost this time. Sharleen's bedroom was decorated in gold—everything. Sheets, lampshade, even the wall art.

"Wow." Hollis chuckled. "I'm just not going to think about it too much." She shook her head and went through the bathroom and into a walk-in closet that was bigger than his master bathroom in his apartment. The one he hadn't been in for a year now.

"Can you get this down for me?"

Will hauled the box from the top shelf and set it on the shiny gold comforter.

"I think I remember…" She flipped the lid off. "A camera. I found this box years ago, and she caught me looking at this vintage camera. Saying, 'she *freaked out*,' would be a serious understatement."

Will took the camera out. "Looks like a bunch of photos with it."

"She didn't have a safe. I think this is as close to hidden secrets as you're going to get."

He'd read the tech's report, but she'd seemed sure when she'd made a beeline to this box. He was going to have to trust her, despite the lingering questions he still had, having just recently changed his mind about her being West, or believing that she'd been involved somehow, someway. Now she just handed him this evidence on a platter? Could be an intentional misdirection. Could be a peace offering.

Will needed to shake off the distrust and just see where this was going. After all, he'd asked her to help him get something concrete, and that was exactly what she'd done.

"Briar?"

Will twisted to the sound of his name being yelled up the stairs.

"That's Savannah." Hollis shuffled papers in the box.

He went to the hall. "Wilcox?"

She trotted up the stairs. "Conroy said you were up here."

"Anything from the neighbors?"

"Apparently, Sharleen and Frankie sped away in her car looking freaked, like they were running from something. Or someone." Savannah said, "How about you guys?"

Will gestured towards Hollis, who had a photo in her hand. "Anything interesting?"

"Huh?" She blinked. "Oh, hey Savannah."

The detective came around him to peek over Hollis's shoulder. "Your mom?"

"I guess. Though, for all I know, this is some random little girl in the desert."

"Looks like New Mexico, or maybe Arizona." Savannah looked at the box. "There's a National Geographic in here, and a couple of other magazines. And...whoa." She lifted out a paper. "This is an award."

Hollis read over her shoulder. "For photography?"

"Sharleen Malta. That her maiden name?"

"I have no idea." Hollis glanced at him, then looked at the magazines. "She's listed on the cover of this. The award-winning photographer."

"This award is for significant contributions to the Vietnam peace initiative."

Hollis frowned. "What on earth—?"

"There's a Vietnam connection with some of the founders of Last Chance. The former police chief, the fire chief, and a doctor who worked in town." Savannah said, "Maybe your mom knew them. Could be that's how she wound up in Last Chance in the first place."

"You think her mom is a founder?"

Savannah shrugged in answer to his question.

"It would set a few things straight, that's for sure."

Hollis continued looking through the box. "Mementos. Envelopes of old negatives. Letters…I think this is from her mom. My grandma."

Will motioned with his fingers, and she handed it over. Then she pulled a blank envelope out and slid the note from it. "Rich Tathers."

Savannah said, "Mia's father?"

Hollis shrugged one shoulder and read the card aloud. "I'll tell everyone what you did."

Will looked up from the letter Sharleen had received from her mom. "She was being cut off. Your grandmother was refusing to give her any more money. Told her to get help. And a real job."

"My grandmother?" Hollis said, "She never said anything about grandparents. Apparently, she was too busy blackmailing people." She passed him a photo. "This was with the note."

The image featured Rich Tathers and a young woman.

"Put it back." Savannah gathered everything. "This all needs to be logged. But there's also no point dragging up the past. I'll talk to Rich. Find out what this was all about, before I take it to Conroy."

"Because you want to protect him, and Mia, from the truth?" Will didn't like that idea. Nor did he like the idea that Conroy or Mia might try to squash something. If Rich had committed a crime, then that needed to be addressed. Right now, they had no idea what was in front of them, so they had to tread carefully.

Savannah shot him a look. "You do your job, and I'll do mine. Okay? Unless you need *another* case to investigate."

"My mom was blackmailing people," Hollis said. "But that doesn't make her West."

Will nodded to concede the point. "Could be she knows who is, though."

"You thought that about me, and you were wrong."

Will pressed his lips together.

"I'm going downstairs."

He moved to follow her, but Savannah snagged his elbow. "Just one sec."

He waited.

"If Rich did something, and it's not outside the statute of limitations, it will be addressed. It's not going to be swept under any rug or ignored because Mia is a lieutenant and the police chief is going to be his son-in-law."

"Good. Now I need to be with Hollis."

"Mmm."

"What's that supposed to mean? Someone tried to kill us earlier. Of course, I'm going to do what I can to protect her."

Will walked out, not willing to leave Hollis exposed to any more danger than she already had been.

The front door was open.

"Hollis?"

He glanced around downstairs but didn't see her, so he went out onto the front step. Hollis was halfway down the drive. About to leave without him? Hadn't she heard him talk about keeping her safe? He should be protecting her. That didn't mean leaving herself exposed with him still in the house.

"Wait up one sec—"

A car engine revved. The sound of gunfire rang out as a dirty white pickup barreled down the street, past them. A semi-automatic pointed out the window.

Hollis's whole body jolted, and she hit the concrete.

15

"Hollis!"

She didn't move, despite Will's cry. Hollis just kept herself as close to the ground as she could. Ridiculously exposed. Nothing but the concrete of the drive around her. Not even those two plant pots she'd gotten for her mom that one Mother's Day to decorate the front step. The ones her mother had never set out. They were in the garage, the flowers dead.

Car tires screeched.

More shots rang out. So many she had to clamp her hands over her ears.

Hollis's injured wrist slammed against the side of her head. She cried out, bile rising in her throat while her arm throbbed under the tight bandage.

Will fell to the drive beside her. "Hollis." He squeezed her shoulder. "They're gone."

She lifted her head. "Donaldson."

"What?"

"The officer over there." She sat up, pointing with her good hand at the curb where the officer was parked.

"He's down."

She pressed her lips together, hardly able to say it.

"I'm going after them. Get to Donaldson." Savannah ran past them, jumped in her car, and sped away with a screech of tires.

Hollis clambered to her feet.

"Easy."

She shook her head and grabbed his hand for something to cling to, tugging Will over to the police car. Her ears were still ringing. She saw Donaldson before she heard him. In fact, the short pants of his breathing almost didn't even register in her brain.

Will shifted. A second later, he said, "Officer down." He paused, then gave whoever was on the other end of his call her mom's address.

Hollis tuned it out and crouched by Donaldson. His face was pale, probably too pale. Blood coated the side of his hair, but she couldn't see a wound.

He blinked at her, his eyes glassy. Shock and fear registered on his face.

"Hey. It's okay." She touched the buttons of his shirt, over his sternum, and tried to find a bullet wound. All she found was extra padding under his clothing. "You're wearing a vest."

"Of...course." He coughed between the words, and then winced. "Hit my head diving."

Hollis nearly sagged to the ground in relief.

Will crouched. "Conroy is on his way, as are EMTs."

"I'm never gonna live this down."

"You think he'll care?" Will asked. "He'll be glad you didn't get shot."

"I agree." She had to say it, even though Donaldson clearly didn't feel the same. "Conroy isn't going to demote you for getting hurt. Right?"

She didn't demote her employees for blunders at the diner. The fact was, people made mistakes. As someone who'd never received that consideration from others, Hollis actually thought it was important to give grace to the people around her. Surely Conroy was that kind of boss. If the police chief was a tyrant, or someone who played favorites, people would be quitting all around him. Or at least they wouldn't be happy.

Instead, everyone who worked with him appeared both happy and completely loyal. Which was what she'd seen in both Stuart and Kaylee.

Was that why Kaylee had gotten so mad when Hollis announced she was leaving town? It hadn't occurred to her to let the people she knew in on her plans. Stuart might technically be her employee, but they'd never hung out outside of the diner.

She didn't know what to make of it. What she did know was that she had no answers, and her wrist hurt. *A lot.*

She hissed and sat her behind on the ground. It might've been more like falling, but she was a lady, so she pretended it happened on purpose.

"Okay?"

She shook her head at Donaldson's question. "I'm more worried about you having a concussion."

"You took a pretty hard spill." The cop's eyes softened.

Will said, "Yes, she did. Because she went outside *without me.* When I clearly told you that you should be under protection." He shot her an unhappy look. "Believe me now?"

"I didn't disbelieve you before."

She didn't get the chance to say more. Conroy raced over, along with Basuto and several other cops she didn't know. An EMT and Will helped her up. They walked her off to the side while the cops did their "brothers in blue" thing.

"*Ouch.*" She whirled to the EMT, taking her hand from his grip.

He held up both hands. "This needs an X-ray."

"I already know it's broken."

He frowned at her.

"I'm not going to the hospital." She only realized afterwards that she'd yelled in his face.

Will motioned away with a jerk of his head, effectively dismissing the guy. Hollis shot the EMT a smirk. Until Will touched her elbow. "Let's go sit down."

"I'm too mad to sit."

He tugged her away nonetheless, making it known in a gentle but firm way that she definitely didn't have any say in the matter. So, when he slowed his pace as he closed in on her mom's porch, Hollis turned to him. "What?"

Will lifted his brows.

She sighed. "Sorry. But she never even put the pots out."

His head jerked and he looked behind him, frowning. "What are you talking about?"

"My *mother*." Hollis didn't even want to go there. Ugh, it was just so cliché. *She never loved me.* Didn't matter that it was true. "She treated me like crap. Now, when I try to get out of her life for good. Which—hello—she should be happy about it, right? No-o. She drags me right back into the middle of it."

Hollis realized then that tears were rolling down her face. "Why can't they just leave me alone?"

"Who?" There was a guardedness to his gaze. As though he felt there was something she'd withheld, which she might be just about to tell him.

Too bad she knew squat about what was going on, past the fact her mom was apparently in the middle of it.

"Those guys from the woods. Whoever just shot at us." She sucked in a breath. "Do you know—she never even told me she was a photographer? I had no idea. And she's won *awards*."

"Holl—"

"Don't bother. Whatever you have to say, it's not going to make me feel any better."

Will chuckled. Then he pulled her to him, so that her face smashed against his shirt. Not saying anything at all.

If he asked her if she felt better, Hollis would just deny it.

She could feel his chest shake against her cheek. "There's nothing funny about this."

"You're very cute when you're mad. This doesn't bode well. If we argue, I'm liable to laugh." He pulled back. "Or want to kiss you."

Hollis stared up at him. "If you're trying to distract me because my wrist hurts, I think it's working."

She saw the humor materialize in his eyes. It drifted across his face to curl up the corners of his lips. The transformation was like watching a piece of pottery emerge from a kiln.

"You guys okay?"

Will tightened his arms for a second before he let her go, but not too far. They faced Conroy together, Will's arm around her shoulders, her body tucked tight against his.

Conroy said nothing, but his expression was clear he found it both amusing and interesting the way she and Will were standing.

"My mom is a nightmare. Other than my life being in shambles, and my broken arm? I'm fine."

"Sure." Conroy's lips twitched. It didn't have anywhere near the same effect on her than when Will did that.

She should be thinking about Phil and how mixed up her feelings were. She didn't know this Will guy. And yet, everything about him felt familiar. There was literally not enough space in her brain to think about it. Nor was there time.

While they chatted about more cop stuff, Hollis realized she needed time on top of that to consider Rich Tathers. His name had been brought to the surface of this investigation. Conroy's future father-in-law. Would Conroy protect the lieutenant's father? Maybe Conroy even knew something had happened between Rich and Sharleen.

Blackmail. Just the idea her mom was embroiled in something like that, on top of everything else, made her sick.

Hollis sighed. She didn't want to consider that they might be dirty cops. Or at least that they played favorites and swept things under the rug—which may seem like less of a deal, but it still meant they weren't the honest law officers she'd thought they were.

Will said, "Savannah went after the truck. It was too fast for me to get the license plate." He glanced down at her.

"I didn't either. I just hit the ground."

Will gave her a small squeeze. "Good."

She didn't know that she agreed with his assessment. Maybe there was more she could've done. "I don't think I helped."

"But you're safe."

That was relative, as far as she was concerned. "I still think leaving is the best option."

She wiggled out of Will's hold. For her to convince him, she needed to be able to argue her case. Which she couldn't do while distracted by his presence. His strength so close to her.

Hollis lifted her chin. "I don't want to be dragged in the middle of this. I want to be as far from these people as possible."

"And when they follow you?"

"That's why you'll go with me. Right?" She wasn't backing down. If Will wanted to protect her, they could compromise. It didn't have to be solely on his terms.

"You know the plan is to stay together."

"And if I don't want that to be here? Would you leave town with me?"

Will opened his mouth, but he said nothing. He'd have to give up trying to get more and more evidence to give his boss, or whoever it was that was coming here to receive it.

He'd have to keep her safe at the cost of finishing this case personally.

Conroy said, "I have a question. Before you guys leave." Like it was a foregone conclusion.

She did like the idea that he might be on her side.

Will mushed his lips together.

Conroy said, "Any idea how we can find your mom?"

She sighed. "I have no idea where she would go. It's not like we hang out. And apparently I don't rate high enough to know even the first thing about her."

Both of them started to object. But Hollis wasn't interested in either of them trying to convince her otherwise of what she knew in her heart to be true.

Her mom considered her nothing.

Less than nothing.

She held up a hand. "Just give me a second. Let me think about it."

Hollis turned away and pulled her phone out of her purse as she took a couple of steps away. They spoke low behind her. Holding the cell was just reflex, mostly. A source of comfort. Familiarity, or habit, didn't matter.

She scrolled to her mom's number in her contacts and dialed it. Who knew, maybe she would pick up. Hollis could just ask her where on earth she'd gone and what was going on.

"Is someone's phone ringing?"

Hollis spun around.

Basuto looked at Hollis and thumbed over his shoulder toward the open front door. "Sounds like it was left inside."

Hollis strode there. Will got to the door first, and said, "Hold up."

He went in, emerging again a few seconds later to show her the phone. "Your mom?"

Hollis hung up the call. "Yes."

"Any idea what the passcode is?"

She tried a couple of combinations she remembered from years ago, when her mom first got the thing. Two wrongs, and then she hit on the right answer.

"Bingo." Will grinned. "This is good. This is seriously good, Hollis."

Conroy said, "He's right. We can get evidence from this that might help us."

It was the "might" that got to her. And the fact her mom's

phone being left here meant they couldn't use her phone's GPS to find her.

Hollis sighed. It felt like this was never going to end. Her mom was going to keep being her selfish self, while she was be caught right in the middle of it all.

The chump with no clue.

16

Conroy reached for the cell phone. "I'll get this..."

Will stepped back. An involuntary action, but Conroy caught the meaning nonetheless.

"That's evidence, Briar."

"It's also my case."

The police chief frowned. "You're gonna fight me on this? My office has the tech to get everything from this device, and your way will take longer."

Sure, that sounded logical. Until you threw in the very personal angle of the note in that box they'd found stuffed in Sharleen's closet. The one that was clearly addressed to the police chief's future father-in-law.

"Why are you hesitating on this?"

Will needed an answer, fast. "I'm just thinking everything through. She left the phone for a reason. Or she forgot it." He shrugged. "Likely, if there was anything useful on here, then she would've made sure to take it with her."

Hollis looked like she wanted to either be sick, or pass out. Neither was a good prospect. He needed to get her out of here so she could sit. Which meant he should wrap this up with Conroy quickly.

"I guess we'll find out."

Will said, "I guess so."

Just like Conroy was going to find out his fiancé's father was mixed up in the middle of this. Time would tell what the police chief, and his department, did with that information. In the meantime, however, Will was interested enough to go to the source and find out for himself.

Will handed over the phone.

Out the corner of his eye, he saw Hollis glance at him but didn't respond to it. Conroy shouldn't know there was something they were keeping from him. That wasn't necessary. It would skew the results of this experiment.

No, it wasn't honorable to play the police chief just to test whether he was on the level. But Will didn't know of any other way to see what a man would do when pushed far enough. If he'd hide the truth, or if he would put his feelings aside and do what was right.

The way Will hadn't done.

"I'm going to drive Hollis." He didn't want to lie, so he neglected to mention where they were headed.

Conroy turned to her. "Are you doing okay? Do you need to get checked out at the hospital?"

She shook her head, but Will could see pain in the lines around her eyes. "I'm good going with Will."

He said, "If anything happens, I'll make sure she gets help."

Conroy clearly wanted to say something. Will lifted his chin, but inside he was just exhausted. Conroy was really going to keep making him prove himself? Even after *everything* that had happened, and all the ways Will had pitched in around town?

He knew it was futile to expect that one day he would be free of the constant battle to show everyone he was good, and capable. That he could get the job done. This was a fight that would last for the rest of his life.

Still, he could imagine. It would feel like a level of freedom he'd never experienced, not even once.

The kind of feeling he got when Hollis leaned in, and he could wrap his arms around her. Keep her safe.

Conroy motioned with the phone. "I'll let you know first what Ted finds on here. Okay?"

"Thanks." Will was trusting them in a serious way. If Conroy was a particular kind of police chief, then he should be seriously worried. As it was, Will settled on mildly concerned—which meant he'd be contacting Eric and explaining it all to him.

Will turned and led Hollis toward his car. "Are you *really* all right?"

She slid her good arm in his, wrapping her fingers around his bicep to hold onto it as they walked. He slowed his pace a fraction. She squeezed his arm, hard. "Do you really think he'd go so far as to protect Mia's father if Rich has done something wrong?"

"I don't know." He hoped not. They stopped by the passenger door. "What do you need, Hollis?"

"I feel like I was put in the dryer on spin. Just without the heat."

Will winced. He got her tucked in the front seat and trotted around to the driver's side. When he was belted in, he turned to her. "I'm sorry about everything. If I'd known how hard this would be, I'd have thought twice about bringing you here. I'd have warned you so you weren't so blindsided."

In none of that had he said he wouldn't have brought her. Something he knew she picked up on.

"You're just doing your job," she said. "And when it comes to my mother, I've learned to roll with the punches. Especially since usually they're flying toward my face."

"She hit you?"

"More like slaps. But not many times."

Will clenched his abs while he pressed his lips together. If he lost it, she would know. Then she'd think he was pitying her, as she had when they were inside the house.

"Didn't you say the back of your head was flat, your father having slapped you upside it so many times?"

Will nodded. "That doesn't make it right." He said, "On the other hand, why do women do that?"

"What?"

"With a guy, you duke it out. After that, there are no hard feelings, because it's been settled."

"By fighting."

He shrugged. "Women can be…vicious."

"Abuse can go both ways. It's not just women who are victims of domestic violence."

He said, "I've seen it. It's a sad fact. But when there's a child involved, one who can't or doesn't know how to defend themselves?" He didn't finish.

"I can hold my own."

"Because you're strong?" he said. "Or because she forced you to learn how to survive?"

"Does it matter? It kept me alive, right?" She nudged his shoulder with her good hand. "And strong enough to face you when you arrested me."

A little levity to break the tension? That was a good thing as far as he was concerned. "I really thought you were West. I didn't want you to be, but I was really sure."

"Because of my mother."

Will talked as he drove. "Do you think she was behind convincing you that Frankie had been kidnapped?"

"I want to believe she wasn't. But to be honest, the fact they're cooperating with each other? That they're now on the run with each other? That's far more unbelievable to me than a fabricated kidnapping story meant to convince me his life is in danger." She sighed. "Though, why would she need me to leave evidence at the diner that points to me and criminal conspiracy?"

"To distract me?"

Truth was, he'd totally fallen for it. West had delivered Hollis to him on a silver platter, and Will carelessly swallowed it all down, whole.

"But someone was working against her," he said. "Because, while it might not have been as much as a surprise to the criminal element in town that I'm an FBI agent—someone outed me —they did burn down the diner."

"And why would they do that when I was supposed to leave evidence there?"

He nodded. "Then, when I leave with you to take you in—which is what your mother ostensibly wanted—we're run off the road and nearly killed by the same guys from the diner."

"So, she's on one side of it, trying to get me arrested. Someone else—maybe West?—is on the other side, trying to stop you."

"Which means she's not West, and if she knows who is, then she might actually be at odds with him," Will said. "And I might be able to get her to agree to testify."

Hollis nodded a few times, slowly.

Will reached over and squeezed her knee, not really sure what to say. He parked by the fence behind Rich Tathers's lake house. In the spot where he'd heard that the police chief's patrol car exploded a few months ago, when Rich was still a lieutenant and his now lieutenant, Mia, wasn't a cop here in town yet. Before Conroy and Mia fell in love with each other and took down Ed Summers.

Will had been right there through all that, playing his part of rough-biker-guy working for hire.

It felt like years had passed since then.

And he still wasn't finished.

Will climbed out. Hollis walked beside him, around the house to the front door that faced the lake. Above the door was a balcony and garden furniture. On the lawn in front of the door, someone had constructed an arbor. For Conroy and Mia's wedding?

The door opened. Rich lifted his brows. "Hollis."

"This is Will Briar."

"Ah." Rich said, "The FBI agent Conroy mentioned."

"Among other things," Will said. "Can we talk to you?"

"Let's go inside."

He led them to the living room. The whole place had a "mountain cabin" feel to it. Woven rugs and log furniture that hadn't been changed in years.

Rich lowered himself into a chair that seemed to envelop him. Hollis took a seat on the couch, and Will stood over by the wood burning stove.

"I'm not gonna like this, am I?"

Hollis said, "It's not good, I'm sorry to say. It has to do with my mother, and a note we found in her closet." She paused, then said, slowly and somewhat dramatically, "I'll tell everyone what you did."

Rich shut his eyes. Then he ran his hands down his face and let out a long exhale. "I've done things I'm not proud of. Had... dalliances, and cut corners in my business."

Will said, "And she found out?"

"Tried to bribe me. Get me to take a job for next to nothing."

"What job?"

Rich said, "Building the diner."

Hollis sat quietly. Will didn't like it, but they still needed answers. "Was she working alone, or did she take orders from someone?"

Rich glanced at Hollis. "I'm just... I'm sorry for all this." To Will he said, "Sharleen is an enforcer. When she wants to be."

"She works for West?"

Rich shrugged. "Pretty sure she works for whoever she feels like working for."

Hollis nodded, a knowing look on her face. That sat right with Will also, so he didn't press hard on that subject. Rich's information could be old. The truth, different now, or the same.

"Do you know who West is?"

Rich glanced at him. "You think if I did, I wouldn't have told my daughter or the chief of police?"

"Fair enough." Though, some people in his situation might have kept the information to themselves.

Before Will could ask another question, Rich looked at Hollis. "I'm sorry."

She kept her expression steady. Resolved. Will didn't like that she felt the need to be so strong. She said, "For what?"

"Meena. Your mother. A lot of things."

Rich's youngest daughter, Meena, had worked for Ed Summers while Will had been undercover with them. That couldn't be what Rich referred to.

"It was high school." Hollis said, "Meena is...Meena."

Will agreed with that. Much like Sharleen, Meena was a law unto herself. No one could pin her down. Especially not since she'd left town months ago. Will hadn't thought she belonged in that life, but if there was a connection with Sharleen, perhaps she'd been drawn in somehow.

"As with my mother," Hollis said, "we both know I have no sway there."

Will asked, "Do you have any idea where Sharleen and Frankie might go if they were to hide, somewhere they could lay low?"

Rich blinked. "Do I even want to know why they're together?"

Hollis shrugged.

Will said, "I'm hoping to find out."

Because it would lead them to West, right? And in the meantime, he would continue to keep Hollis safe. Not like at the house. There would be no more gunfire, if he could help it.

Rich stood, groaning as he moved. "I'll write down a couple of addresses, places they might go that are under the radar. But I don't want anyone knowing it came from me. Not *anyone*."

Will nodded. So many secrets in this town, and he had to

figure out the truth. There had to be a way to solve this case *and* protect Hollis at the same time. There had to be. And Will was going to find it.

Just like he was going to find West.

17

Rich handed her the paper he'd written on. Hollis didn't want to know who he'd noted, or where he thought her mom would go with Frankie to hide. Part of her wanted to tear up the paper and leave town anyway. Let them have their drama. Make them clean up their own mess.

But would the woman she was trying to become—the one desperate to start a better life—become someone she actually wanted to be around?

Hollis had only ever had one thing that was hers, and that was herself. She was who she decided to be. She made the decisions she wanted to make. Cared about the people she wanted to care about. The honor intrinsic to those decisions was in part the reason she'd stuck around for so long, trying to do good in Last Chance.

If her final act here was leaving Sharleen and Frankie behind and in danger, when there might be something she could do to stop it, she wasn't sure she could live with herself. Especially if they didn't make it out okay.

"I..." Rich hesitated. "I guess I'm just sorry. That's all."

Hollis didn't have the mental energy to get into a lengthy discussion about regrets. Still, she didn't want to leave him feeling bad. She touched the outside of his arm with her good hand, and said, "Aren't we all."

She gave his arm a squeeze and let her expression shift to something she hoped looked a whole lot easier going than she felt. "I feel like I've been apologizing my whole life. Mostly for my mother's behavior. Now she goes and...what? Fakes Frankie's kidnapping? Now they're on the run and dealing with who knows what else? Something I obviously have no idea about."

Except that it was part of a plan to single out Hollis as being West.

Will had fallen for the ploy to make her out to be West, and she hadn't even had to put the files on her computer. It seemed like the minute Ted had seen the files, it had been obvious to him they were fakes. Maybe she should take comfort in that. It was a poor attempt to frame her.

Knowing that didn't make any of this less confusing. Hollis had long since given up hope she'd ever be able to think the best of her mom—or even remotely less disappointed. But it still stung. Every. Time.

She was aware of Will behind her. Hollis refused to be distracted by that right now. She was sure she looked like she was daydreaming. She had wondered what he thought of her life, but what did it matter when she planned to walk away from her life anyway? The moment she could do it without feeling regret, she would be gone.

"The cavalry is here."

She turned to find out what Will meant. The front door opened. "Ah."

The police chief, wearing his suit, walked in, followed by Mia—Rich's daughter. Neither looked happy.

"Conroy. Mia." Hollis used her "waitress" smile, the one she pasted on when she had to work, even when she didn't feel good. She also tucked the paper into her purse.

Will touched her back, between her shoulder blades. "We

were just leaving."

"Right." She headed for the door with Will right behind her.

Conroy said nothing about the now-obvious fact there was something they'd neglected to tell him. He looked mad, but Hollis didn't think it was directed at them. Not much of it, at least. Seemed more like the brunt of it was aimed at his future father-in-law. Mia didn't look much happier.

Before stepping outside, Hollis glanced back at Rich Tathers. But when she couldn't think of what to say, she yielded to Will's nudging and walked out. She felt bad for Rich. Who wouldn't? He'd obviously been cornered by Sharleen and the leverage she had over him. Another victim of her mother's selfishness. Kind of like how Hollis had been. Discarded when she wasn't useful, used when it was advantageous to Sharleen.

"You okay?"

Hollis shrugged. They rounded the house, and she saw Conroy's work vehicle parked behind their car.

Will's fingers touched hers. He wound them through hers, holding her hand, stepping closer in the process, so their bodies touched as they walked. Not for the first time, it struck Hollis that even as tall and stocky as she was, Will was bigger. Enough that she felt almost…dainty beside him. A feeling she'd never experienced before.

Safe. Secure. Protected.

Usually she felt like she didn't fit, and not just because of her size. Or her body image issues. Who didn't have those with the constant bombardment of the media's idea of perfection, which was fake anyway?

She figured it was at least in part because of how her mom had treated her in regards to her appearance, versus the truth of her stature in comparison to others. Compared to her mom, she was huge. Compared with regular folks with their normal lives, Hollis was…nothing special. Plenty of people were taller than her. Plenty were bigger, or heavier, than her. She was healthy. What exactly did she have to complain about?

People in Last Chance were nice, for the most part. Probably like any other small town and not some anonymous big city. They weren't the reason she was leaving. Hollis had to face the fact it was her mom she was trying to get away from. Not the rest of the town residents. She also liked her job, even with the constraints. Every job had frustrations and challenges. But she still liked it.

"Where to?"

Hollis buckled her seatbelt.

"What did Rich write down? Because I figure wherever we're going, Conroy and Mia will likely be right behind us."

That was probably true. "Conroy, at least."

"How's the arm?"

Hollis scrunched up her nose.

"Sorry."

"It's not broken," she said. "And as far as I can see, you don't need to feel bad about it. You've saved my life plenty of times today. Yesterday. Probably before that, too, and I didn't even know it."

"Kind of like how you saved me from burning to death in the diner."

Hollis sighed.

"Want to grab a cup of coffee?"

"That actually sounds really good." Still, she said, "Not that I'm trying to avoid getting ahead of Conroy."

"I can take a picture of the note and text it to Conroy."

She eyed him. "Why would you do that?"

"Because you're hurt. Because I'm one guy, and he has police backup."

"Drop me off." She wanted to go with him. But not if she would be a liability. That wouldn't be smart. Neither would it feel good, knowing she was only slowing him down. "You could go with Conroy."

Will studied her. "After the last couple of days, I'm not in a hurry to let you out of my sight. Seems to me like we're doing pretty well looking out for each other. Right?"

She had to admit that was true. "Doesn't mean I have a gun to back you up. I want to find Frankie and Sharleen, but not if you don't think me being there is a good idea."

There had been enough danger. Hollis wasn't interested in just wading into more without careful consideration.

"Unless you have an extra gun?"

Will said, "You know how to use one?"

"Frankie took me to the range sometimes. Mostly pistols, nine-millimeter, a twenty-two, and a forty-five. I don't like rifles. Or semi-automatic anything." Just remembering the sound of one of those made her shiver now. A single shot from a handgun was loud enough.

"Huh. Well, then."

"Does that mean you're going to give me a gun?"

"No."

She twisted around to argue the point with him, but her elbow slammed against the back of the seat and pain flared in her wrist. She shut her eyes and took a few long breaths. While she did that, Will started the car and drove away from Rich's house.

He headed into town, which meant he drove past the diner. Hollis fought the lump in her throat. The front windows were shattered. Inside looked black, the structure little more than a hollow shell of what it had been. Even though the destruction had been mostly in the back of the building, it still seemed like the whole thing would have to be torn down.

She wanted to say something, but what was there to say? Will reached over and squeezed her good hand. There was nothing better he could've done. "Thanks." She tried to think what she was thanking him for specifically, and ended up adding, "For everything."

He squeezed her hand again, then let go.

"I really appreciate you letting me hang out with you." She

had the note, but also knew he would ask her for it if needed, and then meet up with Conroy to do that cop thing they all did. Hollis wasn't required to be part of it. She was just grateful she wasn't alone. He was here, working his undercover investigation. Catching West.

"I'm looking forward to being done with this case." There seemed to be more to it than just those words, but that was all he said. Hollis's contentment deflated like a balloon letting the air out. He only wanted to be done with his job. And with Last Chance. She'd also planned to leave, so she understood it. But hearing he basically couldn't wait to get out of here? She could admit that stung.

Her life made zero sense right now. She felt as though she was being pulled in a hundred different directions. Still, Will was here for the moment at least. She could enjoy it.

But, she knew she could rely on someone even bigger, and even more reliable, than Will. *I guess… thank You.* God hadn't been a huge factor in her life—but she did believe in Him. It seemed to make so much sense that He was up there, running things. Once in a while, something would go her way. Mostly it didn't.

Granted, things could be so much worse than they were. Hollis was grateful for that. And God had sent Will. Sure, he'd tried to arrest her, but through that, and for this short time, it meant they were in the same town, and he was here. Will was with her now when she really needed someone. *Thank You for that.* It wasn't because she deserved to feel better. Or that she'd earned any kind of reward. Still, she'd been given the gift of protection when she needed it, and a way to feel good about herself while her mom did whatever she wanted, regardless of who she stepped on.

Sharleen's actions shouldn't affect her, but they did. And in spite of her mother's selfishness, God had given her a good man in the middle of it all. Maybe they could help each other.

"When we get to the coffee shop," she said, "I'll give you

Rich's note. You can go do your thing. Get this done."

Will pulled into the parking space and frowned at her. "If that's what you want to do. It would be safer than wading into danger."

"I didn't wade in earlier, and I was still hurt." She lifted her arm, even though it was painful. The sling was helping some. A sick feeling in her stomach was replaced by rumblings of hunger.

"Come on."

They headed inside, and Hollis avoided looking at anyone at the tables. Or behind the counter. There were plenty of people in here, hanging out. Kids. Moms meeting up over coffee. Two guys doing a Bible study. Three men in office attire, talking over printed pages and a tablet.

She turned to Will. "I have to use the restroom. Can you get me a mocha?" She started to reach into her purse.

He put his hand on her arm. "It's fine. I got it."

"Oh." She smiled. "Thanks."

"And a sandwich?"

"Yes, please. The chicken salad is really good."

He smiled. "Better than yours?"

"Where'd you think Margie got the recipe from?"

He laughed, loudly enough several people turned to watch. Hollis just grinned and headed for the back hallway, where the bathroom was.

She took care of some pressing business and then stepped back out. A hand grabbed her bicep on her hurt arm.

Hollis yelped. It would've been audible, but a huge hand covered her mouth and muffled the sound. He dragged her back. All the way through the EXIT door at the end and outside, where he slammed her against the wall.

Hollis gasped for breath. His face swam in front of hers, unfamiliar, but she understood immediately that he was dangerous.

"Where are Frankie and Sharleen?"

18

One barista put Will's sandwich in the toaster oven. The other steamed milk. But the sight of all that regular, everyday activity didn't settle him the way it normally did. He turned and studied the coffee shop. Could be there was a reason he was so restless. Maybe there was someone here that he knew in his persona as a local biker thug. Instinct pushing him toward self-preservation.

But there was no one in the coffee shop he recognized. And no one seemed inclined to pay him any attention—overtly or otherwise.

Will stowed his phone without replying to the email he'd received from Eric right before hopping into the rental car at the airport. His boss was inbound, and it wouldn't be long until he got here.

He moved to the hall. No one there. Exit door at the end, one staff door and the two for the bathrooms. Single occupancy. He didn't check to see if the doors were locked. If Hollis was busy, she didn't need to be bothered by his disquiet.

Will paced all the way down the hall, noting the artwork. Also, trying to put his finger on the instinct or inkling he'd been given from Whoever was watching out for them. It was so indiscernible; he hardly knew what to do with it.

From outside, he heard a muffled cry and a thud. He quickly shoved his hip against the bar on the EXIT door, and looked outside. He gasped. "Hollis."

She slumped against the building. Will rushed to her and caught her before she landed on the ground. Across the lot, an older, white compact bumped the curb and turned onto the street.

Arms around her, he tucked her against him and looked down to speak in her ear. "What happened?"

A shudder moved through her. She had been dealing so well with everything, he'd wondered if she really was all right. Was this the blow that would break the dam, making Hollis realize her entire life was in shambles?

She'd lost the diner.

She'd lost her family relationships.

Thanks to him, she'd almost lost her freedom.

"I'm sorry I arrested you." Her body jerked at his words, and, except for the groan that escaped her lips, he'd have thought it was a result of a laugh. His phone rang in his pocket. "What happened?"

"He shoved me against the wall." She sucked in a quick breath. "He took the paper."

And then took off in a white car.

Will pulled his phone and sent Conroy a text. He gave her an assessing stare. "Are you hurt?" As soon as he asked the question, Will realized what a dumb question that was. She was obviously still hurt from before. "Any more than you were, at least." Maybe she'd hit her head.

Hollis shrugged. The action was stiff, but it didn't seem like she was any worse off than she had already been.

"I can get an ambulance. Or drop you off at the doctors."

Something washed over her face, but it moved too fast for him to catch what it might've been. She pulled out of his arms.

"I'm fine. If you want to drop me off somewhere though, that's fine."

"You think I'm gonna let you out of my sight now?" The minute his back had turned, she'd been threatened again. Hurt, again.

"I might've argued that I'm fine going to the bathroom by myself, which is what I was *trying* to do. But I guess we've proved that's incorrect."

"Hollis—"

She shook her head. "Don't. Just give me a second." She lifted one hand, palm to him.

"What was on the paper?"

He hadn't read it, but had seen her look it over. Surely she remembered what was on it.

Hollis glanced to the side.

"Do you think you can give a description of the man who attacked you?" He pulled out his phone. They'd need mug shots, or a sketch artist. "We can show it to the guy we picked up before. Find out who he works for."

Hollis slapped the phone out of his hand. It landed on the ground with a crack that didn't sound good.

Neither of them moved.

"Can you just stop being a cop for *one second*?"

"I thought you were fine." The second the words slipped out, he realized it was the exact wrong thing to say.

"I am *fine*."

Will didn't even touch that one. His phone buzzed. "That's probably Conroy telling me he's sending someone here to open a case file."

"I'm not a victim. My life isn't a police case."

Will pressed his lips together. While that may be true, *his* life most definitely was. For years it had been nothing but a series of cases and investigations, and would continue to be until he quit undercover and worked behind a desk. Or until the day he retired from the bureau, dressed in an uncomfortable suit.

Before he could say anything, a cop car rolled up and Sergeant Basuto climbed out. "Hollis." He walked straight to her. "Are you all right?"

She nodded, looking like she was about to cry.

Will wanted to give her another hug. His phone rang, and he swiped it off the ground. She'd shattered the screen protector, but the glass screen under it seemed to be intact. He peeled off the protector and tossed it aside. "Briar."

"I'm pulling into town." Eric said, "Where are you?"

Will told him what had just gone down.

"She all right?"

He sighed. "Seems to be."

Will turned away while Basuto spoke with Hollis.

"I'll be there in ten."

"Copy that." Will hung up. More cops arrived. Uniformed officers, and the chief. Mia, the lieutenant. Savannah, the detective. He repeated the same short description of what happened over and over until he was sick of saying it. Until the barista figured out what was going on and brought out his sandwich, then made coffee for everyone there.

Hollis went back inside with the barista, leaving Will to watch her walk away. Again. The last time that happened, she'd been attacked. This time, he had to sip his coffee and not look like a crazy man who just wanted to secret her away and keep her somewhere safe. She needed to feel like she had autonomy. That was better than feeling powerless.

Yes, he still needed her help to finish this. Only in part because he owed her more than a simple apology for ever thinking she was part of this. He'd been blind to the truth. Too determined to close the case and get out of Last Chance while he could still breathe.

Now he just wanted to be where she was. To finish the case and see where this thing between them might lead.

Could be whatever was growing between them would fizzle

to nothing, never to be. Or Hollis could meet him halfway, and they would be each other's last kiss.

Right now, he didn't know. But Will sure wanted to find out.

"Briar!"

He twisted to see Eric Cullings, FBI Special Agent, trot over to him. The man wasn't a stranger to Last Chance. In fact, he was brother-in-law to the town's private investigator—who was himself married to the detective, Savannah. Small towns were worlds in their own right.

"Where is she?"

Will thumbed over his shoulder. "Inside." Safe. There were plenty of people in there, so nothing would happen to her. Not this time. And if he could help it, not ever again. Until this was done, work would come first. Which meant he was now doubly determined to find West.

"And the parents?"

"Either Hollis or Rich Tathers need to tell us what was on the paper that got stolen from her. Then we'll have our lead back."

Eric folded his arms. "I'll talk to Conroy." He turned and waved the chief over. "Whoever was on that list could be in danger, and it'd be good to get ahead of them. Warn whoever it is that may be caught in the middle."

They conferred with Conroy, who nodded. "Rich gave me the same list." He looked at his phone screen. "Davis Fermium. I don't think I know who he is. And the manager of Highway 44 restaurant, Liam Athens."

"I've never heard of Fermium either. Pretty sure I'd have remembered that," Will said. "Athens's name came up before. He owns the restaurant?"

Conroy nodded. "Local businessman. I've never had any contact with him aside from at his place of business. The pie is real good." He cracked a smile.

Eric said, "It really is."

Will was partial to the dessert at Hollis's diner. Before it'd been burned down with him inside, that is.

Conroy said, "He actually also owns the diner under his company. Which I didn't know. He owns several businesses in town."

Will frowned. "The restaurant owner also owns the diner, his biggest competition? And that's never struck you as being strange."

"Can't say I've ever looked him up before." Conroy said, "No reason to dig into the life of someone without probable cause."

That was true. If the police chief had no reason to suspect a man of anything, he couldn't very well put that person under a microscope. Or, at least, legally and ethically he couldn't. Some cops might. But not Will, or any that he cared to know personally.

He said, "I'll go grab Hollis. See what she can tell us about him."

Conroy's brows lifted. Before Will could walk away, the chief said, "And after you've squeezed her for information, what then?"

Will didn't know what to say.

"My suggestion? Give it to God."

Will said, "I'm supposed to do what now?"

"Give it up to Him."

"What?"

"All of it. The case. You and Hollis. The future."

Will blinked. "Pretty sure I can take care of that myself."

Eric made a noise like he thought Will's comment was amusing.

Conroy said, "Sounds familiar." He glanced at Eric. "I thought that myself. Until I realized I needed Him to help me. Now it's as easy as breathing to ask for God to do His will."

He'd always thought God's will was a funny phrase. Even back in the third grade when his grandmother had called *him* that. Then she'd died, and he hadn't wanted much to do with a God who would take away from an eight-year-old the only good thing in his life.

Conroy patted him on the shoulder.

Will didn't wait for permission to go after her, he just went inside and down the back hall to the coffee shop. He looked around but didn't see her. At the front window, he scanned the lot. Wanting to vocalize his frustration, he spun around instead.

Eric was right behind him. "Where is she?"

"I don't know."

"This isn't good."

Will bit back what he wanted to say and pulled out his phone. He dialed Hollis's number, but she didn't pick up. A second later, he got a text. As though she'd done some kind of automated reply, not wanting to answer the call.

Can't talk.

"What'd she say?"

Will shook his head. "Nothing. I'm sure she's fine, and maybe just left in her car. I'm sure she didn't get kidnapped. Which at this point, would probably make more sense, given everything else."

"Conroy is right, you know?" Eric shrugged. "You kind of should give it to God."

"You too?"

"I didn't know where you were at with all that. My bad that I didn't ask."

Will said, "Not a workplace conversation normally. Especially when I don't check in much for fear of blowing my cover. The people I'm usually pretending to be aren't exactly the church type."

"Briar!"

He and Eric both turned. Conroy headed back to them. "Basuto hit the restaurant for his lunch break. He just called in asking why Hollis is over there yelling and making threats."

19

If she'd actually thought this through, Hollis would have gone somewhere and found a gun to bring with her. Not to actually shoot anyone with. But waving it around would have helped make her point.

She faced off with the waitress—a woman she'd fired a few weeks ago for skimming money from the cash register. As though Hollis wouldn't have noticed she was short money.

"Just tell me where Mr. Athens is, and I'll be happy to get out of your face."

The waitress smirked at her. "All you're gonna get is arrested."

Hollis turned around. Basuto stood outside, holding his phone to his ear. Probably calling Conroy, or Will, or any one of the other cops in this town. Hollis didn't need him getting in the middle of this. As much as she respected any of them, the tough job they did and the badges they wore, she had to figure this out herself.

Hollis moved to the door and threw the deadbolt. It wouldn't keep him out forever, but it might buy her a minute or two. She turned back to the waitress. "Tell me where Athens is. *Now.*"

A flicker of concern washed over the other woman's face. Letty, a bleached blonde cash skimmer. Hollis figured if there was illegal activity going on here, then the woman she'd fired was probably part of it.

She opened her mouth to ask *again*, when a rough-looking man emerged from the back. She swallowed what she was about to say and watched him stalk to her.

"What do you want?"

"To talk to Athens. Obviously."

The man needed a haircut and a shave. He also should put his clothing in the laundry and wash out the dirt smell.

She said, "Is he even here?"

"Nope." He folded his arms across his chest. "He ain't here."

"Let me back there." She motioned to the hall. "I'll check for myself. If he really isn't here, then I'll leave a note."

They weren't going to stop her from confronting him. There was a reason Rich Tathers had mentioned Athens on his note. Clearly Rich thought there was a link between him and Sharleen.

Hollis couldn't help thinking about that. *Don't go there.* But it was inevitable.

Liam Athens owned the diner, as well as this restaurant. She'd never liked him. Considered him more of a necessary evil than anything else. But if she'd wanted to be part of the diner, then she'd had to deal with the fact Athens was the money behind Frankie's business.

But right now she needed to know of his connection to Sharleen.

"No way I'm letting you back there."

Hollis figured as much. "Not good enough. Get him on the phone if you won't let me leave a note. I'm not walking out of here until he talks to me."

"I'll tell him you stopped by." Letty shifted her head side-to-side, all attitude. Like Hollis was gum on the bottom of her shoe. "I'm sure he'll call you."

"Not good enough," Hollis repeated.

Hollis had never thrown her weight around. It wasn't like she had any authority. Unless it was with people who worked for Frankie. He'd let her run things for a while. Athens sat behind the scenes, Frankie pulled the strings, and Hollis was the puppet.

It was time to cut herself free.

"Get him on the phone." She stuck out one foot. "I'll wait. After all, the diner just burned down. There are things to talk about. Like insurance, and what we're going to do moving forward."

That was a good line. But it made her wonder...that is, until her thoughts were cut off by the rattling of the front door handle. Basuto.

In all the bluster she had, there was a kernel of truth. If Athens was involved, then he could be the one behind the fire. Or behind the flash drive that was supposed to implicate her. What if *he* was this West person—or even the mastermind of the whole persona.

She still wasn't sure West was a real person. Or even just one person.

Maybe it was a group. Why not create a persona for the police to hunt while the real people did whatever they wanted while no one was looking for them? Athens could have planned for her to go to jail. The police would stop looking for "West," and he would be able to get the insurance money from the diner fire.

Basuto knocked on the glass door. "Open up right now."

Because Letty looked like she was about to start a fight? Hollis was probably the one who would wind up getting arrested. And all because Athens might be West. He wasn't even here to answer for himself.

Letty moved.

Hollis braced, but the woman strode past her and went to let the sergeant in.

"This woman is disturbing our customers."

"I just want to leave a note," Hollis told him.

The rough guy huffed under his breath. She twisted to glare at him. Why did Athens have a thug here, anyway? This guy looked like someone Will might have met undercover, and he was here when Athens wasn't. A customer, or a hire? Not restaurant staff, given he was far from clean. He was more like a mercenary.

She would know, considering she'd met several bad guys for hire the past few days. The kind of man who might've tried to burn down the diner with Will inside. All to hurt a good guy, a federal agent.

This rough man was exactly kind of guy her mother would see as strong, though he was nowhere near a nice guy. Not like Will.

Hollis wasn't like Will either. She was stained with her mother's world, and with her connections to all of these people. Sergeant Basuto was on Will's side of that fence. Hollis didn't like where she was.

Which was exactly why she'd planned to leave town.

Why stay here, and be this person, when she could start over somewhere else? She could be clean. Like Will. Do the right thing and make the right choices, because it was who she was and not because it was the only way to feel good about her life and who they'd made her to be.

"Hollis, let's go talk about this." Basuto motioned for her to move aside with him.

"Liam Athens might've destroyed my entire life. I should have the chance to ask him if it's true."

"This is a police investigation, girl." Basuto at least appeared to have some compassion. Unlike anyone else in her life. "The truth will come out. But not with you in the middle of it."

"I can't get out of the middle of it. They won't let me." He had to understand.

She wanted to pray that he would, but this was hardly the time to bend a knee and bow her head—even proverbially.

"Let's talk."

Hollis was about to explain why she was *done* with all the craziness when the door opened again. She spotted movement behind Basuto. By the time she realized what was happening, the sergeant's body jerked, and he slumped to the floor.

Behind him stood her mother.

Her mother turned to her, swung the gun around and aimed over her shoulder.

Hollis said, "No—"

The gun fired. A blinding flash, a deafening shot, like a firework going off right in her face. She spun, ears ringing, and saw the thug on the ground directly behind her with a red, wet stain on his chest. He was dead.

"You killed him!" Hollis's outcry was drowned out by Letty screaming.

Sharleen swung the gun around. She didn't fire again, just wacked the waitress in the face with the gun. Letty hit the floor.

"What are you *doing?*" Hollis didn't even know where to start.

Sharleen pulled Basuto's gun from his holster and tossed it toward her. Hollis caught it on a reflex, then stared down at the weapon in her hands. "What are you—"

"All right everyone!" Her mom yelled the words loudly enough so that every patron in the restaurant could hear. Thankfully the place wasn't overly full. Sharleen called out, "Cell phones and wallets on the table in front of you. No one calls the cops, and no one moves."

An older man wearing a Vietnam vest stood.

Sharleen pointed her gun at the ceiling and fired. "No one moves. Do as I say, and no one gets hurt."

The man sat back down, beside his wife. Two kids sat across from them. Grandchildren?

Hollis shook her head. "What are you doing?" There were innocent people here who could get hurt.

"Frankie is in the car. Get the money out of the register, and let's go."

She just stood there, staring at her mom. Unable to believe what was unfolding. "You killed a guy."

"If you knew him, you'd know that's no loss." She gave Hollis a look, like she should know that. "Get the money and all their wallets, and let's go." When Hollis didn't move, she said, "Chop chop. Cops will be here soon."

Sharleen walked up and down the aisles, collecting people's wallets and shoving them into some woman's purse she had confiscated moments earlier. Hollis didn't know what to think. Her mom was here, Athens wasn't. A man was dead, and the sergeant had been knocked out. Hollis didn't want to be an accomplice to armed robbery.

She needed to subdue her mom, but didn't want to get into a gunfight with her own mother. Not with the added risk that an innocent bystander might get hurt. "Why are you robbing this place?"

"To get you back. Obviously."

"I don't want to be part of this." She looked at Basuto. He was out cold, a sheen of blood in his hair.

"You've got no choice. So, get the money and make this look good. Or do you want me to hand you over to the cops again?"

Hollis pressed her lips together.

"Athens deserves this."

"These people don't." There had to be another way to do… whatever her mom was trying to do. "Let's just go."

"Get the money, Hollis. Are you stupid? Because if you wanna be, then I'll shoot you myself."

Someone gasped.

Neither Hollis nor her mother broke their locked gazes to

look where the sound came from. *You'd really shoot me?* The look in her own mom's eyes said very clearly, *yes*. She should have been surprised. Maybe she was, in part, since she'd never thought her mom might kill her. Or that she'd even want to.

"Just go."

Hollis didn't know who that was, but she agreed. "They're right, Mom. Let's go."

"Get the money from the register." Her mom shoved past her to look out the front window.

Was she really supposed to make herself an accomplice? She would cross a new line, stealing. She didn't want to be even an accessory.

Sharleen turned back to her, lifted her gun, and put a bullet in the artwork behind Hollis. She flinched. The squeal was involuntary. She dropped Basuto's gun.

"Why are you doing this?" Hollis had to ask. She needed to know. Liam Athens wasn't even here, and her mom was determined to stick it to him. To hurt a cop, and shoot a man. Hollis even felt bad that Letty had been hurt. Though she didn't have any reason to feel that way.

She was supposed to be fixing this, and now it was worse. Instead of getting answers to prove she had nothing to do with West, she was now part of an armed robbery? Her life was officially out of control.

"Let's *go*. Now." Her mom looked like she really wanted to shoot Hollis. A look she'd seen before, only this time, Sharleen held a gun pointed at her. Finger on the trigger.

Hollis turned the key in the register and the drawer slid open. She grabbed a handful of the largest bills and strode to her mom. "You go. I'm right behind you."

Sharleen would step outside.

Hollis would throw the deadbolt and put the money back.

"No way." Her mom grabbed her arm. "I came in here for you. Now you're coming out with me."

20

Will pulled up beside Basuto's squad car. Another car was parked in the lot with the engine running. The same car they were seen taking off in from Sharleen's house. Frankie sat in the front seat.

The second he saw Will, Frankie hit the gas and pulled out.

Will headed for the front door of the restaurant. Six feet from the door, it was pushed open. "Hollis."

He took in the expression on her face, then saw the wad of cash in her hand.

"What are—"

"Back up!" The woman behind her screamed the words at him.

Hollis was shoved forward. Her mother was right behind her, standing in the open doorway. As though she couldn't decide whether to come outside or retreat back into the restaurant.

Will pulled his gun and aimed it. He'd shoot Hollis, or possibly someone else inside the restaurant in his attempt to hit Sharleen. But he was ready. Just in case. "What are you up to, Sharleen?"

Hollis was shoved forward again and this time let out a small whimper.

"She's already hurt enough. Just let Hollis go."

Sharleen sneered. "I do what I want with my own daughter."

"Yeah, that's not how this works." While his heart squeezed in his chest, he said, "Let her go, Sharleen. She's been through enough."

"I have." Hollis spoke through gritted teeth. "Just let go of me, *Mom*. Enough already."

"No."

Will backed up. "Step out of the restaurant, Sharleen. Whatever you're trying to do is over."

"I'm *trying* to save my daughter."

Will shook his head. He figured this was a case of, 'I brought you into the world, I can take you out.' Except this woman was just unhinged enough to take that literally. And she had the gun to back up her threat.

Hollis looked incredulous. He didn't blame her. Sharleen was trying to save her by holding her against her will and threatening to kill her? This hardly made sense.

He said, "This isn't the way to do it. Put your gun down, Sharleen. I'll lower mine, and together we'll figure this out."

She jerked Hollis and pulled her backward through the door. Sharleen yelled, "Get back! All of you, get back!"

She stumbled. So did Hollis. Someone lay on the floor. *Basuto.*

Sharleen yelled, "Lock the door!"

Before it could swing shut and Sharleen could get her wish, Will stuck his foot between the door and the frame. He pulled the door open and headed inside.

Someone said, "Now there's three of them!"

A couple of kids were crying.

Will yelled, "I'm FBI. Sharleen, put the gun down. Now." He kept aim on her as she dragged Hollis back toward the hall.

What she didn't do, was put her gun down.

Before she disappeared, Will crouched quickly and pressed two fingers to Basuto's neck. After finding a faint pulse, he straightened and continued moving with them. Sharleen was retreating.

He wasn't willing to let Hollis out of his sight. It hadn't worked well before, and he had a feeling this time would be no different.

"Mom, don't do this."

"I'll kill you." Sharleen had to have a grip on the back of Hollis's jacket, or her belt. She jerked Hollis, who let out a cry.

"You're hurting me. But of course, you don't care about that at all, do you? You only care about yourself."

"Shows what you know. I wouldn't be doing this if not for you."

"Like it's my fault?" Hollis asked.

Her question made Will wonder if she was stalling her mom long enough to give backup more time to get here. And while he was pretty sure they weren't all that far behind him, Will couldn't risk waiting for Eric or the Last Chance Police to show up.

He had to do this himself. The way he knew he had to finish this case if he ever hoped to have the chance to talk with Hollis about how he felt. Now that knowing was far stronger, and he'd doubled down on his resolve. He knew, here and now, that Sharleen was a serious risk. If he wanted that chance with Hollis, this was how he'd get it. By sticking with her and saving her life.

"There's no reason to hurt her." Will was prepared to turn the tables and stall her as well. She didn't need to leave, and there was no way he would allow her to go anywhere with Hollis. "Let Hollis go. You leave, and I'll tell the Last Chance Police you got away."

Hollis blinked at him. Her face was awash with fear, the visceral knowing that things were bad. Seriously bad.

Did she believe her mom might actually pull the trigger and try to kill her? Or was she simply scared for Will's life? Perhaps the fear he was seeing on her face was actually for him. Because she cared, and even though he turned out to be someone very different than Phil, the man she'd thought she was dating this whole time. She still that didn't want to see him get hurt.

Sharleen huffed. "All this is for Hollis." She reached around and snatched the cash out of Hollis's hand, then stuck the wad of bills in her back pocket.

Hollis turned in the same direction as her mom's retreating hand and shoved at her mom with the flat of her good hand. Her mom slammed the gun into the back of her shoulder. Hollis faced Will again, and he could see the pain in her eyes. "Why are you doing this? Just leave me alone."

He'd heard that from her before. This time, like previously, his heart squeezed in his chest. He felt her pain. "Let her go." The words cracked on their way out. Will felt the gathering tears burn before they blurred his vision. "I will shoot you. Just let her go."

Before Sharleen could answer, the door at the end of the hall opened. Liam Athens walked in, a big man with a sturdy build and dressed in a suit and tie. Will thought he looked out of place in a small mountain town.

"What's going on?" He glanced between Sharleen and her gun, and Will, holding his outright.

Sharleen sneered. "This is *all* your fault! Get out of the way."

"Are you kidnapping your own daughter?" Athens looked at her like she was so far beneath him, that he was baffled she'd even made it this far in life. "What is wrong with you, Sharleen?"

"Put the gun down," Will said. "Before anyone else gets hurt." He motioned for Athens to move out of the way, past the two women, so that he could take shelter behind Will. Out of the line of fire.

Sharleen waved her gun from Will, and then back to Athens. Tears rolled down Hollis's cheeks. "Let's just go, Mom. You don't have to do this." Despite her words, she looked at Will. For hope? Seemed like she thought he would save her, regardless of whether she went with her mom or not.

"She's not going with you." Athens said, "Let her go, Sharleen. This is beyond ridiculous." When she didn't move, he said, "I was told you were robbing me. Now you're kidnapping. You should give up. In minutes, there will be a sea of cops right outside that door." He pointed a thick, long finger at the exit. "Just waiting to kill you the second you step out. Do you think they'll let you hurt Hollis?"

The woman herself seemed surprised Athens had said that.

Sharleen screamed. "You think *I'm* the one who's gonna hurt her? I'm saving her from *you*." She wailed every word, loud and high pitched, so it was hard to even discern enough of what came out of her mouth to understand what she was saying.

"Sharleen, let her go." Will gritted his teeth.

"Mom, do as he says."

"Sharleen, you're doing this to yourself." Athens sounded so high-and-mighty, along with his obvious disappointment.

His stature, alongside Hollis's, made Will pause. They were both taller than average and stocky. He couldn't study their features, but there was something about the tone of Athens's voice that reminded him of Hollis's alto tone.

"Is Athens your father?"

Hollis gasped. Sharleen whirled around. She squeezed the trigger of her gun and a round hit the wall, high above and to the side of his head.

Will flinched.

Athens said, "Enough." The restaurant owner tackled Sharleen against the wall. She screamed. Hollis cried out, high and full of pain.

Two seconds later, a gun went off.

Athens backed up and slumped to the ground, one hand

clutching his shoulder. Blood seeped through his fingers. He called Sharleen a vulgar name.

She screamed, "I'll kill you!"

Will couldn't take her down. He didn't have even an inch of a clean shot in this tight hallway. And no way would he risk hitting Hollis.

He'd have to wrestle the gun away from Sharleen—a move that meant Athens took a bullet to the shoulder. "Let her go, Sharleen."

"Kill her!" Athens yelled.

Hollis cried. "No! All of you, stop!" She tried to twist around to her mom, but Sharleen wouldn't let go of her broken arm. "Don't do this, Mom. You're hurting me. Just let me go."

Her mom's grip on her meant Will couldn't pull her from her mom's clench without seriously hurting her. So that kind of tug-o-war was ruled out.

Think. He had to take her mom down. *God, I need You.* Was that what Conroy had meant, about giving it to Him? Will had been to church a few times as a kid. He'd even gone to Bible camp once at fifteen. He'd learned more about girls than Jesus, if he was honest. But some of it had stuck.

You're the one who needs to save her. He couldn't do it on his own, that was for sure. This was a big admission for him, as he'd never enjoyed the life of an agent that involved a partner at his side. Will worked far better alone. Except when the operation moved out of his control.

You have control of everything. I remember, and I believe that. So, help Hollis now. Give me what I need to save her.

Athens yelled. Hollis screamed. Her mom dragged her to the door and forced Hollis out first. Too close. A bullet would go through both of them.

Will followed as they stepped outside. A second later, he heard the ratchet of a shotgun. "Get down!" The call out was instinctual, though he didn't dive to the floor. Will slammed his body low against the outside wall of the restaurant, aimed his gun, and found the source.

The vehicle he'd seen Frankie in.

Will fired a bullet at the front tire. It embedded itself in the quarter panel just above the wheel well. He grunted in frustration, then called out, "Sharleen, let her go!"

The shotgun fired.

Will had to dive out of the way as buckshot sprayed the wall behind him. He fired a shot in reply, and saw Frankie slump down in his seat for cover.

Will fired at the car again, aiming for anything he could hit that would slow them down. Police sirens rang out, and probably an ambulance, as well. Time was running out.

He got to his feet, spread them, and lifted his weapon. Will started to squeeze the trigger.

The door behind him swung open, and Athens barreled out. He slammed into Will, sending his shot wide.

Will fell to his knees. Athens landed on top of him, rolled, and lifted his hand to shoot at the truck.

"Cease fire!" He was going to hit Hollis.

Will got up and ran toward the vehicle as it sped away, praying God would give him the speed to jump on the trunk. They would undoubtedly fling him around. Who cared, when he'd be with Hollis? The cops would see him and follow. They'd help him get her out of Sharleen and Frankie's grasp.

Athens never stopped firing.

Will pounded two steps toward the vehicle. It was close enough, he knew he'd be able to do this before they got too far away.

A bullet clipped his side. Will took another step and tried to ignore the fire whipping like lightning through his hip.

His leg gave out.

Will tumbled to the ground and lay there listening to the engine roar.

Hollis was gone.

21

Hollis's heart screamed. The sound emerged from her mouth, until her mom clamped a hand over it.

"Shut up."

Hollis shoved her hand away.

Frankie was in the front, both his hands gripping the steering wheel. His right leg was nearly useless, so he drove with the left one. It had never seemed safe to her.

"Just stop the car. Pull over."

Sharleen said, "After all the trouble I just went through to get you out of there? You're crazy." She leafed through the bills Hollis had grabbed out of the cash register. "And all for a lousy two hundred forty bucks?" She sighed.

Hollis leaned over and screamed in her face. "Will just got shot!"

Sharleen shoved her away. "I'll shoot you, too, if you do that again. Ungrateful girl."

"This is a nightmare. What on *earth* is going on here? You just robbed the restaurant. Frankie, the kidnapped victim, is your getaway driver. And for all we know, Will could be *dead* back there!" She gripped the hair on the sides of her head and tugged, determined to pull it out. Only that could compare to the agony rolling through her.

Sharleen grabbed the two front seats and climbed over the center console to land in the front seat, leaving Hollis alone in the back.

She dropped her gun into the cup holder like it was nothing. Like she hadn't just robbed a restaurant at gunpoint and kidnapped Hollis.

"*Let me go.*" She screamed the words at both of them, and kicked the back of the seat. Then she sat back, breathing hard.

Sharleen shot her a look. "So ungrateful."

"Are you trying to insinuate, in your own little *way*, that you did me a favor? Because I'm not seeing how any of this can be a good thing." She didn't have her phone. Was Will okay?

Fear for him rolled through her. That he was hurt. Dead. Injured. Bleeding. Not breathing, no heartbeat.

A whimper escaped her throat.

Now he was gone, and she'd never get to tell the big, rough man that he was *everything* she'd ever wanted. In a best friend. A husband. A lover.

All the work he'd done was for nothing.

The case would never be closed.

Tears rolled down her face.

"You never did see." Her mom was on her phone. Muttering her words, not engaging with Hollis any longer. "Always thought more of yourself than the rest of us."

She wasn't even going to touch that. Her mom's opinion of Hollis, and what she thought Hollis's opinion of her was, made zero sense as far as she was concerned.

"Frankie." Hollis wasn't even sure what to say. "Please. Just let me out. Pull over, and I'll go. I don't want to be here."

They'd kidnapped her. Her mom, and the man she'd always considered a father.

"Your mom is right. You should be quiet." He twisted his grip on the wheel and didn't look at her.

Because he was ashamed? She didn't know. "You were supposed to have been kidnapped. Now you're here. With *her*."

"We're all okay. Things are okay."

He said nothing else. Hollis twisted to look out the window. If the cops were following, that would be a good thing. But no one pursued them.

They were probably dealing with Will's dead body. Still laying where she'd seen him fall.

Hollis swiped at her face with her good hand. The other arm, she hugged to her body, trying not to dissolve into uncontrollable tears at the way it hurt. Her mom had grabbed her. Hauled her around. Taken her from Will, who'd been there to save her.

So much for Hollis's plans. Now they were less than useless, and they hadn't started out being all that good in the first place. She'd tried to confront Athens. Look how that turned out.

Is he your father?

Will's words rolled through her head. She squeezed her eyes shut. *One thing at a time.*

"Why are you doing this?"

Her mom lowered her phone with a long sigh. "You really don't know? Darlin', this whole thing is your fault."

Hollis seriously disliked the way she called her darlin' with that sneer in her voice. "My fault?"

"Well, you ruined all our plans after you got arrested. So, we had to improvise. Armed robbery makes the biggest statement. With any luck, that FBI agent will think you're a criminal again and arrest you. Again."

He's dead. "Why do I need to be arrested? You're the one who tried to frame me as West, right?" Hollis leaned forward. "Why pretend you kidnapped Frankie and get me to plant evidence that I'm West? Is it you? Are *you* West?"

Sharleen rolled her eyes. "Like it's that simple?"

"Then why don't you explain it to me. You owe me that

much, getting me arrested like that." Not to mention trying to do it all over again with your shenanigans back there.

"I owe you nothing. Everything I've ever done was for you."

Hollis let out a short, sharp laugh that sounded utterly humorless. "You only ever think about yourself. That's been clear to me for as long as I can remember."

"Yeah? That how you remember things?"

Hollis didn't know what to say.

"Shows how little you pay attention. Or how well I kept you from seeing the truth about my life. Helps that you were convinced you were the center of the universe."

Hollis pressed her lips together.

Her mom continued, "Turns out you know nothing. Not about me. Not about Frankie, or the diner either."

"You mean like how you had those guys beat Will and try to burn him alive in the diner?"

"Sure. That was definitely me." Sharleen shot her a look. "I don't have hired thugs that work for me. It was Athens, Hollis. He's been behind everything."

"He's West?"

Sharleen let out a frustrated sound. "It's not that simple! Athens has been controlling this town for years. He used you as leverage, and he even caused Frankie's accident because Frankie refused to let Athens launder money through the diner."

"That was you who wanted to do that." Hollis had been sick at her mother's aspirations to be a criminal. Now what was she supposed to believe?

Her mom said, "Athens shattered Frankie's leg, because we wouldn't do what he wanted. It was the last straw. I've been trying to get out from under his thumb ever since. So that we can finally be together." She touched Frankie's leg.

He didn't seem super receptive to her affection, but Sharleen wasn't paying that much attention. She said, "Everything I've done has been for the diner. For all of us." She included Hollis in that statement.

"What are you talking about?"

"I've been trying to *save us* from him."

Frankie's jaw clenched. His knuckles were white on the steering wheel.

"Then we'll be free, and we can finally have the life we wanted."

Despite the hope in her mom's words, it appeared that Frankie didn't necessarily feel the same way.

Hollis sat in the back, aghast, while her mom continued, "You don't wanna know what he was going to do to you. And I didn't want you to live my life, so I saved you from him."

"By pretending that Frankie was kidnapped."

"Athens is the one who taught me about leverage." Sharleen said, "Now he can't get to you, and I'll destroy everything he has so there are no photos left."

"Photos of what?"

"Me. Obviously." Sharleen shook her head. "You don't wanna know what I did for him."

"He put you in a compromising position?"

"And made me his mouthpiece around town. Without that, I'd never have been able to raise the cash to finally get away from him."

"Like armed robbery?" Hollis pressed her lips together as soon as the words were out.

Her mom said, "He runs this whole town. Everything I did was because he forced me to do it."

Frankie inhaled a deep breath and pushed it out. "You've been working for Athens this whole time?"

Hollis couldn't begin to understand how he felt. The suffering he'd been through. Was there anything left of their relationship? Her mom seemed to think there was. Frankie, though? She wasn't sure about him.

"Now what?" Hollis really wanted to know. Her mom clearly had a plan. "Where are we even going?"

"Somewhere Athens won't find you before we get out of here."

"I have an interview to be at."

Sharleen shook her head, laughing a humorless laugh. "That 'interview' was *Athens*. So it didn't look strange when you suddenly disappeared. That's why I had to intercept you."

Frankie said nothing.

Hollis didn't know what to say either.

Sharleen shrugged. "I just want to be free of all this, you know? Start over somewhere else. A place no one knows me, or my history. Where they have no clue the things I've done. The person I've been."

Hollis squeezed her eyes shut, her tears dry now. "I was packed and about to leave town when I got the message that Frankie had been kidnapped. I would already have been gone, if it wasn't for you. None of this would be happening."

"Except that Athens planned to grab you before you could leave. We had to get in there first to keep you from being taken by him."

"Is he my father?"

Frankie stiffened. Her mom said, "No. His brother is."

"And where is he?"

"Dead now."

Hollis held herself completely still. "And you saved me from Liam Athens."

Sharleen said, "You don't wanna know what he'd have wanted from you. Even if you are his niece. He doesn't care one whit about anyone unless he can use them."

"You don't know what he'd have demanded of me?" Hollis wasn't sure her imagination could think of anything worse than what her mom had already done. And the pain in her arm was getting to be too much. She was having trouble processing all this, and it seemed like Frankie was just getting angrier and angrier at her mom.

"Probably he wanted the diner, and that meant getting you

out of the way. So he could burn it down and collect the insurance money. Which he still did, anyway."

"With Will inside." Hollis needed clarification. "You're the one who got me arrested."

"To get you away from Athens." Sharleen said, "I knew you'd do whatever to save Frankie, and if you were put in jail, then Athens wouldn't be able to get to you. Leaving town wouldn't have been a good option for you. Didn't matter where you ran. He'd have found you."

Frankie exploded, flinging one arm in Sharleen's direction while he said, "So why are we running now?"

"We have to *try*. Otherwise we have nothing." Sharleen said, "There has to be better somewhere else."

There would have been, for Hollis. By herself.

Away from her mom.

But not anymore. Now Will had been shot and was either hurt or dead, and she was back in her mom's grasp, even though that was the last thing she'd ever wanted. All because of her mom's bizarre idea of protecting her.

"I can't believe you did all this. That you can't just let me live my life and leave me to take care of myself." Hollis said, "I'm sorry you thought you couldn't get away from him. But you didn't tell me anything. You never even gave me a chance."

The correlation between what her mom wanted and what Hollis had tried to do was far too close for her liking. She didn't want to be anything like her mom. And here they'd landed on something that almost made them seem like relatives with similar ideas.

Her mom's accusations might prove true. If she'd been a victim Hollis's whole life, Hollis hadn't had a clue. Could it really be true that all her mom's selfish actions were because Athens was controlling her?

What else in her life had Hollis been blind to?

Sharleen twisted around to face her. Before she could speak,

Frankie said, "Don't bother. She's right. You should have told us Athens is the one who was behind it all."

"You didn't know?" Hollis was incredulous. She'd thought he'd been a party to all of it.

"Your crazy schemes. Giving me half the information. I guess nothing has changed, and I doubt it ever will." Frankie pulled the car over to the side of the road. "You've betrayed me for the last time. Which is what I'm going to tell Athens when I kill him, too."

"What are you doing? We have to *go.*" Sharleen glanced around nervously. "Why did you stop? Why are you saying these things?"

"Frankie." Hollis wasn't sure what to say, but she didn't like the look on his face.

He snatched up the gun from the cup holder. Sharleen slammed her hand against his forearm, kind of like the way Hollis had smacked the glass from Sharleen's hand, causing it to shatter against the sink.

Frankie's finger pulled the trigger, and the gunshot went wild.

22

Will hissed. "Ouch." Dean huffed out a breath, all his attention glued to Will's side. "Don't be a baby. It's just a graze."

Will shot him a look he didn't see while Eric and Conroy grinned. "None of this is funny. What was Sharleen even thinking, coming here to confront Athens?"

Conroy said, "The waitress, Letty, told me Hollis pushed her around. Said she knew from the beginning that Hollis was there for the money. And that she didn't care who she hurt." He shrugged. "Hollis fired her a while back, so could be there's bad blood between them."

Eric ran his hands down his face. "Lord, save me from small town politics."

Will didn't know what that meant.

"Had a problem with someone back in the third grade? Watch out. They'll boycott your business for life."

"Okay. But, how does that help us find Hollis?" Sharp pain slashed through his side. Will sucked in a quick breath. "Easy."

"Like I said." Dean taped down the gauze. "Baby."

Will ignored him to pin Conroy with a stare. "So, I gave it to

God." He was aware of the rest of them reacting. Straightening. Body language stilled, as they waited for the conclusion. Will continued. "I mean, what else is there to do? I got shot, and Hollis was kidnapped—by *the very people* who are supposed to take care of her."

That was the biggest issue he had with what'd happened.

Not that she'd gone in alone, or that he hadn't been able to save her—although that hurt. The problem he had with all this was that this was her own mother. Her stepfather—for all intents and purposes. People who should protect her. Care for her. Instead, they'd dragged her into their drama. Implicated her. Left her to fend for herself.

And then, at the end of all that, they'd dragged her back in to do it all over again.

Will continued, "We are not working with rational people here. What can they possibly want with her? Because it feels like she's just this pawn to be handed back and forth whenever they feel like it. Get out of my face. Oh, no. Now I need you back."

Dean said, "Sounds like personal experience."

"It isn't." Will knew Dean was a counselor, but he didn't need therapy. "What it is, though, is my business to watch people."

He was an undercover agent. If he read people wrong, it cost him his life, or at the very least, his case or his standing with the group he was supposed to get in with.

But Hollis's family? They made no sense. There was more to what had been happening than he knew, and he wasn't much closer to unveiling West now than he had been before. When he'd arrested Hollis, thinking it was her.

"Her mom and Frankie won't hurt her, right?" Eric suggested.

Will said, "We don't know that."

Even Conroy didn't look convinced she would be all right. "There's a BOLO out on all three of them, plus the vehicle—

thanks to your description." He twisted to look over his shoulder before the end of his statement and lifted his hand in a greeting. "Mr. Athens."

Will followed Conroy and Eric to the back of the ambulance where Athens was being bandaged. He didn't have the look of someone wanting to field anymore questions. He just wanted to know where Hollis was.

And then he asked, "Why did you shoot me?"

"I was trying to stop them. You stepped in front of me."

Conroy said, "How's the shoulder?"

Athens did look pretty pale. He also looked irritated. "We should be going to the hospital."

"Not so fast." Will didn't care if the man was frustrated. Both of them had been shot, but Will didn't have to answer for anything. He was here doing his job. Which meant taking down Sharleen. "She said that this was your fault. What did she mean by that?"

Will had blurted out his stupid, off-the-cuff question, asking if Athens was Hollis's father. Now that he'd thought about it, there was a serious resemblance between the two of them. Was it true?

Athens shook his head. "That woman is crazy. Always has been. Into one scheme, or another, no rhyme or reason to it. That's why I told Frankie I wouldn't lease the diner to him if Sharleen was involved."

"So, you were behind him employing Hollis. Making her a huge part of the business." Will figured he wouldn't have an issue saying anything against Sharleen, whether or not it was true. Considering what she'd done, nothing would sound outlandish at this point.

There were plenty of witnesses, and Will had seen her shoot Athens. Right before Athens clipped him.

She might have a grudge, but he'd have to agree under oath that she came across as seriously unstable.

"I guess." Athens said, "What does Hollis's employment have to do with Sharleen?"

Will shrugged. "Might not. I was just curious."

"I'm not her father."

"Okay." *My bad.* Only, he thought for sure there was more to it than one simple statement, a denial of his involvement. "Why would Sharleen tell you this is all your fault?"

If it was true that Athens had no dealings with her, how was he involved, then? The idea he could be West floated through Will's head. Right now, he didn't care who West was. All he cared about was where to find Hollis, preferably fast enough she would be unhurt—physically and emotionally—when he got there.

Conroy filled the silence while Athens tried to figure out what to say. The chief commented, "You should know, I have a witness who listed you as a person Sharleen and Frankie might come to if they were on the run. Now I'm thinking it might have been more like a hit list, rather than a list of people who might hide them if they wanted to lay low."

"I wouldn't help them," Athens said. "And that was before she shot me."

Will shrugged. "Why would she try to kill you? What do you know, or what did you do, that means Sharleen came gunning for you?"

"She's crazy. I believe I said that already." The restaurant owner frowned. His attention dropped to Will's neck, and he figured that meant the makeup that kept the spider web tattoo on his neck covered up was coming off.

He'd figured as much, given everything that'd happened. Will used the tattoo as part of his undercover persona. For polite company, he covered it up. Had Hollis seen it? He wondered what she thought of it. But he had to get her back first, if he ever hoped to ask her.

"She's not just crazy, right?" Will said, "She has reasons."

Eric jumped into the questioning, "What do you know about those reasons that might give us a clue into her state of mind?"

Athens swallowed as though there was a bad taste in his mouth. "Frankie and Sharleen think they run this town. They've got a finger on everything that goes down."

"They're that connected?" Conroy asked.

"I thought you were investigating West," Athens said. "Seems to me like you should've heard their names in those same conversations before now."

"I'm beginning to believe West is just a ghost." Will said, "Made up, a distraction so we all chase our tails and wind up coming up with absolutely nothing." He shrugged, lifting his chin. "West is just a name all the criminals in this town hide behind because they think we're too stupid to figure out he, or she, is no one. Or everyone."

For just a split second, Athens's face flashed with surprise, before a bland look of boredom washed over his face. "How should I know? I'm a restaurant owner. That's all."

"Mmm." Will nodded. "Sure. Only, I'm thinking one of those guys back there, unconscious on the floor? He works for you. And I'm also thinking you're the one who sent two guys to burn down the diner."

"Why would I burn down a building I own?"

Eric said, "Insurance scam."

"I don't need the money."

"That's good," Conroy said. "Because you're unlikely to get any after the fire marshal concludes his investigation and figures out it was a job by men you hired."

The chief's phone rang. He stepped away to answer it.

Will didn't move his attention from Athens.

The EMT said, "We're heading out now. So wrap up your questions, guys."

Athens shut his eyes. "I'm done answering already."

"Yeah. No." Eric said, "You're up to your neck in this, and we're going to prove it."

"When you come back with a warrant." Athens pulled out his wallet and handed over a business card. "Then feel free to contact my lawyer. Until then, I have nothing to say."

They backed up, and the EMT shut the doors.

"This case is turning into a giant mess."

Will didn't respond. He turned away and headed toward Conroy so he could get the latest intel. From the look on the chief's face, it wasn't good.

Eric spoke again. "What's the word?"

The chief hung up. "A woman's body was found on the side of the road. She's been shot in the face."

Will said, "Get us the address."

Ten minutes later, they were speeding to the scene. Will directed his FBI handler, while Eric drove with the gas pedal all the way to the floor.

"You doing okay?"

Will glanced over. "She's not dead. It's either someone else, or it's her mom."

"You think?"

"More like I refuse to believe anything else."

"You thought she was West at first." Eric said, "Now you don't even think West is a person?"

"Makes more sense to create a fictitious persona that has the cops all scrambling."

"You're right. It does."

"The head of a criminal enterprise? I'm not thinking that's Sharleen." Will said, "She doesn't have the focus."

"Athens?"

"He was entirely too comfortable. As though he has layers of protection, ways he's covered himself over the years. To the extent that he now considers himself untouchable."

"No one is beyond the reach of the law," Eric said. "Though plenty try to be."

"You think he'll run?"

"Maybe. Pretty big clue he has something to hide if he

does." Eric shrugged one shoulder. "As opposed to staying here and gambling on whatever protections he has in place. So, you tell me—in all your undercover work in this town, you ever hear the name Athens?"

"It's all West this, and West that. Liam Athens is a respected businessman, sure. Is he behind all this? Living large and raking in the cash with intimidation and illegal activity?" Will paused. "He's got thugs at his restaurant and probably hired the ones who burned down the diner. I want a list of his assets so I can take a look at what else he also owns around town. And I want to talk to people who've done business with him. Like Hollis, and Frankie. They know him better than I do."

"Okay. That's somewhere to start." Eric pulled over behind a cop car.

Will didn't unbuckle his seatbelt.

"You want me to go look?"

He shook his head and shoved the door open, got out and strode to the officer. "Got an ID?"

"Female. Brown leather jacket."

Will tried to breath around the lump in his throat.

"Can't determine the age, but she has dark brown hair."

"I need to look."

The cop stretched out his arm, indicating for Will to go ahead. "You really undercover FBI?"

Will nodded.

"Must be some case."

He ignored the rest of what the man had to say and went to look at the body. He realized immediately it wasn't Hollis and glanced back at Eric. "It's Sharleen."

"You think Hollis killed her?"

"Not with a shot to the face."

"Frankie, then?"

Will stood. He shrugged, more to himself than anyone else. Whoever ran the crime in this town, he didn't much care.

Someone else—like Conroy and his cops—could figure that out. They could clean up Last Chance.

He only wanted to get Hollis back.

More than solving the case. More than getting out of Last Chance. His life wouldn't mean a thing if he didn't save her life, after everything he'd done to put her in jeopardy.

Hollis was the only one he cared about.

23

"You shot her." Hollis clutched her broken arm to her front, fingers to her lips. In the front passenger seat, blood coated the inside of the windshield and the side window, which now had a huge crack in it.

Frankie grunted, turned a corner onto Hamilton Street, and pressed the gas pedal down again.

"You killed her. Why'd you do that?"

"Shut up, Hollis."

She pressed her lips together, a hiccup in her breath every time she tried to inhale. "You just threw her out like a piece of garbage." After watching her mom get her head blown off, Hollis had then watched her stepfather reach over to open the door and *shove* her body out of the car. Dead. Lying on the side of the road.

"Where are we going?" Anger wouldn't let her go. The burning rage in her gut made her want to reach over and just… what? Grasp him. Dig her nails in him. She didn't want to be a cliché but scratching his eyes out also wasn't a bad idea.

In fact, it sounded like a very good idea.

"Just let me out of the car." She didn't want to be in the backseat any longer. She had to get out of there. She could barely breathe. *The blood.* Hollis gasped. She could smell it. Even taste it, that rusty tang at the back of her throat. She he wanted to vomit.

"Shut. Up." He drove with one hand on the wheel, one still holding the gun. The murder weapon.

"Let me out." He had to let her go. But he wouldn't, would he? After all, she was a witness to his crime. Frankie was going to kill her.

But then, why didn't he do it already?

She said, "What do you want with me? Why are you doing this? Why don't you just let me go?" Her voice got louder and higher. Until the sound of it hurt even her ears.

Frankie swung back with his arm. The back of his hand and the butt of the gun slammed into her forehead before she could get out of the way.

Hollis slumped against the back of the seat, fingers now pressed to her forehead, while pain screamed through her head and arm. Tears rolled down her face. *He might not be dead, but I will be.* She didn't want to believe Will was dead, even though she'd seen him fall. She'd rather trust Whoever was up in heaven, sovereign over everything, that he was all right. Too bad they'd never get to see each other again, since she would be dead before he caught up to her.

If he was even looking.

Her stepfather drove another half an hour, making a wide circuit around town. Using winding roads. They ended up at a gas station that was a rest stop for truckers, where he pulled up to a pump and used that window cleaner swipe thing to clean the blood off. Even afterwards, Hollis could still see it.

Frankie moved to the pump and started to fill the car. She watched him move, only a slight hitch to his gait.

The crutches he normally used lay on the floor by her feet.

Ones he normally couldn't move anywhere without.

She needed to get out of here. Hollis leaned forward to look in the ignition. No keys. She yanked on the door handle, but on the left side. Opposite from him. *Will he shoot me, too?* She figured the question wasn't if, but when.

Hollis hit the unlock button and stumbled climbing out. She bit back her grunt of pain and got to her feet, then just ran.

"Hey!"

She didn't look back, just raced away. Toward the rows of semi-trucks all parked while their drivers ate a late breakfast and drank several cups of over-sugared coffee. Beyond the trucks was an acre of brown grass where dogs were supposed to do their business.

"Hollis! Stop!"

She didn't. Just kept pumping her arms and legs, pushing pushing through the horrendous pain, and ran as fast as she could with tears rolling down her face, and dripping from her nose. Looking as haggard as she felt.

He was keeping up with her. Probably even gaining on her. But he didn't shoot her as she tried to run away.

Which meant he didn't want to—or couldn't—kill her. Yet.

She rounded the front of a truck and glanced back. He ran like there was almost nothing wrong with his legs. Not the permanently injured man she'd been taking care of for years, and covering for at work. A man who'd needed a wheelchair at the end of an especially long day. Who couldn't walk without the assistance of crutches. And now he was running after her.

Spinning around towards him over the hood of a semi, she screamed, "You lied to me!" And then she twisted back around to keep running—

—And slammed right into a solid man's full belly.

"Whoa, little lady."

Before he could grab her, which, by the way he was moving, was where his hands were headed, Hollis darted around him. Quicker than she'd ever thought she could move.

"You guys got some problem, that's your business..." The trucker guy's final word dissipated like smoke. "Why you got a gun, man?"

Frankie stood at the end of the front of the truck.

Hollis started to back up, not wanting to leave this guy at the mercy of her stepfather. But what choice did she have? "He killed my mother."

The trucker guy glanced half back over his shoulder, not taking his attention from her stepfather. "I don't want in the middle of your business. I just didn't want my truck to get scratched." He took half a step toward his driver's door and reached up for the handle.

Frankie fired a shot at her, over his shoulder. It slammed, instead, into the semi on her other side. Hollis screamed. She wanted to slap her hands over her ears, but could only curl into herself and try to be as small as possible. That only made her think of her mother's words about how *huge* she was, and how it was so obviously a personal failing.

But it wasn't what was going to get her killed.

That was on her mom.

I saved you from him. Sharleen had been so adamant about saving them all from Athens, she'd neglected to see the threat beside her. An angry man who was now intent on cleaning up loose ends. A man who hadn't realized Sharleen had been working for Athens. Until today. Now Frankie wanted to kill them all.

"Just go." She lifted her good hand, palm out. "Leave me alone. I won't tell anyone anything. I'll never say a single word about you, or mom."

"You'll be telling them you killed her."

Because she was the scapegoat? First her mom, now Frankie. Maybe Frankie had been the evil mastermind all along, and she'd just been blinder than she even knew. Or was it that she was so determined to take care of him so she could feel like a good person, that she'd ultimately failed—or refused—to see the truth.

"I'm not going to jail for you."

Frankie sighed. "You'll do what I tell you, Hollis. Now let's go."

He strode to her. She backed up. The trucker moved. As soon as Frankie passed him, he reached for Frankie's wrist and the gun. Two handed. More than she could do. Hollis tried to get out of the line of fire.

She had to duck, crouching low by the underside of the next semi. Could she roll under there and get away? Maybe if she had to. There were a lot of things she'd have thought she couldn't do, and life was proving her wrong in all sorts of ways.

The gun went off.

The trucker's body jerked and Frankie shoved him to the ground. He grabbed her elbow before she could react, and squeezed hard, his thumb stabbing into the nerve as he dragged her back across the parking lot.

Someone stepped out of the gas station store. Frankie waved his gun at the young man.

"No!" Hollis tried to shove his arm down, away from the person.

He flung the passenger door open. "Get in. Climb across, you're driving."

She started to argue, but he had a gun pointed at her. She really didn't want to die. Not when she was just now realizing that she'd been caught up in exactly this for her whole life.

Okay, so not exactly. But if anybody deserved to be overly dramatic at the moment, she did.

Selfish ambition, uncaring actions, and deceit had swirled around her since birth. From both Sharleen and Frankie. Now that Sharleen was dead, and now, also, the trucker, Hollis knew it was inevitable that Frankie would come after her next.

"You don't need me."

"Drive."

She turned the key and pulled out. Her foot slipped off the gas, and they coasted for a few feet.

With his gun still pointed at her, Frankie used his other hand to squeeze her arm until she cried out.

"Okay, okay. I'm going." She clutched the steering wheel. "Where am I going?"

"Drive, before someone calls the cops and they catch up."

She thought that would be a good thing. Why had no one reported them already? Conroy was one step behind them, and he'd get here after Hollis and Frankie were gone. *Will.* No, she couldn't allow herself to think about him. Dead. On the ground.

"Where am I going?"

"Toward Freeline." Then Frankie's phone rang, and he answered it. "Yeah, we're on our way." He listened for a long while.

Enough time for her mind to circle back around to the fact she'd recently been dragged into all this. Fact was, she'd lived in it. Hollis had wanted to be good. To earn love from everyone she cared about, and to prove that she was worthy of receiving it. Instead, they'd been plotting behind her back. Enraptured with their own selfish actions, and what they'd get out of all that.

They hadn't cared about her one single bit. Only keeping her around for someone to use until she'd outlived that usefulness, and they got to throw her away, like Frankie had done with Sharleen.

No, that might not be completely true. Her mom had seemed to think she was at least *trying* to do the right thing for Hollis. But even after a lifetime of musing, Hollis didn't think she'd understood the whole of it.

"Good." Frankie's barked word jolted her from her thoughts. It had sounded like an order almost. He followed it with, "Lock it down. I'll be there in half an hour. I just gotta make sure we're clear."

He hung up the phone.

Hollis gritted her teeth. "I never knew you, did I? Just what you wanted me to see. And my mom?"

"Too busy with Athens to worry about me," Frankie said. "Which is how I like it. Keeps business clean when your personal life stays out of it." He paused. "Can't decide whether to thank him before I kill him, or just shoot him dead."

"Let me go." She didn't want to see another person get killed. There had been enough of that.

"Not until business is concluded."

"What does that mean?"

Frankie said, "Soon as I'm done, you will be also."

More tears fell, even though she would have sworn she'd cried them all out. Apparently, she hadn't run dry yet. Her life was out of control. *Help me.* She needed a way out of this. Even though she'd tried to leave, things were so much worse now.

"I cried for you." She took a breath and said, "I thought you were kidnapped, and I stuck around to help you. So that I could *save* you."

He shook his head. "I never told you to care about me."

"Why are you doing this?"

"Time to get out of town. Only way to do that free and clear is if you're along for the ride, and I wrap it all up neatly in a bow."

"So you're going to blame everything on me. Keep pretending you're injured, too hurt to hurt anyone. That it?"

"It's worked so far. No one even had a clue. Not even you."

Hollis had been managed, kept in the dark and lied to all this time. He'd controlled her. The truth was, she'd let him do it. She hadn't opened her eyes to see the truth. "It won't work."

She wouldn't let it work.

There couldn't be evidence. She hadn't done anything.

"Like I said. No clue." Then he lifted his hand holding the gun. She flinched, but he just said, "Take the next left. We're making a stop."

24

Will said, "Thanks." He turned and jogged back to where Eric stood talking with Conroy outside the gas station. "Maybe half an hour. That's how long since they were here."

Eric folded his arms. "So where would he take her?"

Conroy's attention was on his cops, who were currently with a dead man, investigating the man's recent murder. "Frankie." His voice laced with the hard edge of frustration.

And yet, they'd all missed this.

The police chief scratched at his jaw and shook his head. "Athens said it was all Sharleen."

"Now I'm thinking it was Frankie all along. Maybe she knew, maybe not. They're all using misdirection to throw us off."

Eric said, "Hollis knew, or her mom?"

Will shrugged. "Both. Either. The attendant said Frankie walked fine, maybe just a slight limp." Unlike Will, whose leg seriously hurt even though Athens had only grazed him.

Conroy's eyebrows rose. "But no crutches? No wheelchair."

"Exactly." Will said, "He killed Sharleen. Now he's on the run. Sticking to roads and places they won't be seen by too many locals or cops looking for them." He didn't like lumping

Hollis in with her lying, murdering stepfather, but the fact was, if they found one, they found the other.

Where would Frankie take her?

He'd been undercover as a biker in this town for months. Had met a whole lot of unsavory people. Only, he had to try and remember if he'd ever seen Frankie outside of the diner. Or heard of him where it wasn't all about the tragedy of his accident, and how his life would never be the same again.

But as West?

He'd certainly had the time to be about that bad guy life while Hollis ran the diner for him, because she thought he wasn't able. If he'd been conning everyone all along, then there was likely plenty they didn't know. Frankie had figured out how to live under the radar and fool nearly everyone. He'd hidden a murderous heart and had the deceit to pull off criminal conspiracy.

Will rubbed at the aching spot on his chest—which had nothing to do with his various wounds.

"I'll go talk to Athens again," Eric said. "Ask him about Frankie this time, instead of just Sharleen. See what he and his lawyer have to say."

"Assuming it'll be the truth." Will wasn't so sure it would be.

"Got a better idea?" his FBI handler said.

"Maybe."

Thinking about the places he'd been and the people he'd met while he'd been undercover, made him wonder if he couldn't move in those circles again. Flash Frankie's picture around. Ask about him. Find out where he liked to go. What vices he had. Where he was likely to hide a stash of money or something else that would fund his escape.

"What are you thinking?"

Will said, "I need to go change clothes. And wipe the rest of the cover up off my neck."

Conroy's gaze drifted to the tattoo on his neck. Probably more visible than he knew, since he hadn't looked in a mirror.

"You think you can take Frankie down acting as your undercover persona?"

"I think I can get close enough to get eyes on Hollis and call it in."

Eric slapped a hand down on his shoulder. "You're gonna call for backup?"

"I can be taught."

Conroy barked a short, sharp laugh.

Eric said, "Just one problem."

Will turned to him, but said nothing.

"Those two guys tried to burn you alive? They knew you're FBI. So how do you know you're not putting your neck out there, about to get shot for your trouble?"

How did he tell Eric that he didn't care about the case? Or himself. Just Hollis.

Eric must've read it on his face because he squeezed Will's shoulder and then let go. "It's dangerous."

"So is her being with Frankie. We don't know what he plans to do to her, and the longer I stand around here, the more chance he has to do it."

"Good." Conroy glanced at his phone. "No one's been in and out of his place, so whatever he's doing, it isn't at his home."

That ruled out one spot.

Now Will just had to figure out which of the hundred other possibilities was the one he should try first.

Eric shook his head. "I don't like it. Either Athens or Frankie sent those guys. Means he knows you're FBI."

"I have to do this."

Will walked away before either of them could object.

Forty minutes later, he'd completed his transformation back into biker guy/bad guy and had made a few calls. Seemed something was going on. People he'd worked jobs with, who'd transported narcotics or weapons through town, were quiet. Too quiet.

Will climbed into his car and made one more call, even praying the guy would pick up. He needed to find Hollis. To know she was all right.

"Yo."

Will tried not to sound eager. "What's the word?"

"What do you mean?" The guy sounded cagey. Not a good sign, but given his vices, there could be a number of reasons why this local lowlife sounded like that. It didn't only indicate he knew exactly who Will was. Or why he was calling.

Will said, "Need some cash. What'cha got for me?"

"Quiet night. I'll call you, a coupla days maybe."

"Ah, man." Will dragged it out. "Got child support due. I need somethin'." He sniffed.

The man was quiet for a long minute. Too long. Then he said, "Elm Street. The blue house. I'll have somethin' for you."

Will hung up and drove. *Please let this work.* He couldn't guarantee what he was doing would net a result. And certainly not that he wouldn't wind up being shot for being a cop.

But if there was even a chance it would get Hollis back, then he was glad he'd been extensively trained to do exactly this. He'd worked undercover for years. He knew how to finesse situations.

Eric was right to be concerned about the risk. Which was why Will continued the prayer he'd started. He didn't want to bargain with God, but if it got Hollis back, then he would promise literally *anything* to save her life.

He stuck a gun in the back of his belt, another at his ankle, just in case. Phone in his back pocket, because it would be faster to slide out than if it was at the front. Will wore his bulletproof vest. He didn't care what it said about his opinion of the odds here. He just wanted intel on where Frankie might be, and where Hollis was at.

Will scanned the street for Frankie's car but didn't see it. What he did see was a tiny blue compact with a huge man in the front seat. Tate, a well-known, local private investigator, in a borrowed car. Any other day or time, he'd have laughed at the sight of the big man squashed in that tiny interior, but Tate was here to help. And this whole thing was no laughing matter.

Will was definitely not in the position to turn away Tate's help. He opened his contact list at the name, "Tate." Then locked his phone and slid it back in his pocket. If he had to make a call fast, he wanted the right number on screen as soon as he unlocked his phone.

Will and the private investigator had worked together before. Tate was a solid guy Will would be happy to have at his back.

He knocked twice on the door and let himself in. Jeans. Boots. T-shirt and leather jacket, two earrings and a spider tattoo. He hadn't shaved, so that helped.

"Anyone here?"

"Kitchen!" The reply was slurred. His "friend" had been drinking, or he was on something else entirely.

Will stepped into the room. Quintessential biker, but undercover FBI. Usually he'd try to become the person he was pretending to be, as a method actor did with a part. Tonight? He didn't even bother. The guy was two sheets to the wind. He wouldn't even notice or appreciate Will's fabulous acting abilities. "Whatcha got goin' on?"

The other man had cargo pants on and a threadbare gray sweater. He blinked with yellowed eyes. "It is you." Shook his head and greasy hair fell over his forehead. "Thought I dreamed that call."

He tried to hide that he was reaching for a gun, but Will wasn't dumb. "Don't."

The other man sighed.

Will said, "All I want is information, but if you wanna trade that with the DA for a reduced sentence congruent with whatever I find in this house, that's up to you." He just didn't have long enough to go through the paperwork for an official deal, so he decided to state plain his business here. "I'm not here for you. I just want Frankie."

His head jerked back. "Nah. Nope. You don't touch Frankie." He pushed out a breath and cursed. "I thought this was about those two girls Athens put upstairs."

It is now.

"What I do with Frankie," Will said, "is my business."

"You'll get dead. What do I care?"

Behind the man, on the dirty counter, were several items that indicated what he'd been sniffing up his nose right before Will walked in.

He wasn't unaccustomed to seeing it. But, like every time, it turned his stomach. He'd probably never get used to being this close to people getting high while he had to fake he was doing the same. If he did get used to it, he'd have to quit right at that moment. This life couldn't change him.

He wouldn't let it.

"So, tell me where to find him. He's West, right? Or close enough."

The other man snorted. He seemed to have forgotten he'd just handed Will another whole case, if there really were two girls being held upstairs. The man said, "West. Cracks me up."

"Cause Frankie has the cops all chasing their tails looking for a ghost. Right?"

He smirked.

"Give me Frankie. I'll get you what you want."

Will was a cop, through and through. This was what he'd been born to do. He was the guy who waded into the darkness and dragged the truth out into the light. Whether it wanted to be exposed, or not. His dad might not understand his wildness, but Will knew more now than ever before, that he was exactly the person to do this.

The one to save Hollis from the swill she'd been born into. The selfish ambition and complete disregard for her safety. Sharleen had been bad enough. But if Frankie really was the one they wanted arrested as West, then he was so much worse.

It was hard to say what all Frankie had done, given everything that had been attributed to his name. Will knew for sure that he'd have physical evidence that Frankie killed Sharleen, and Hollis would likely testify to the rest of it.

Slam dunk.

But why didn't that make him feel better?

Right. Because he might be here as an undercover FBI agent, but he was also here as the man determined to get Hollis free of these people. Free of the lies they fed her all those years. Her entire life, a scam.

Save her. He wanted to do it, but it was God who was a sure thing. He was the one to bank on. No question. Will had sung about it at Bible camp. *I believe.*

If God saved her, he'd follow Him. Whatever it took. Faith would be worth it.

"Can't just talk. Make a deal? Can't do that." The man's expression darkened. "Ain't no way I get what I want anyway, so what's the point?"

"Then just tell me where he is. No one will ever know it was you who talked."

He made a pfft sound with his lips, losing some spit in the process. "Think I'm gonna trust a cop?"

Will shrugged. It really had been worth a try. "Where is West?"

"Right here." The voice was female, making his heart sink into his chest.

Because Hollis walked into the room. She was so pale. Hair falling out of her bun, strands tickling the sides of her face. Hugging her broken arm to her front. Blood on her jacket.

Behind her, Frankie. Holding a gun. Looking nothing like the man he'd seen come in the diner. No crutches. No wheelchair. All this time he'd been hiding this?

And now he held Hollis's life in his hands.

Pointing a gun at the back of her head.

25

Frankie used the end of his gun to shove her into the kitchen. Will shifted, his arms opening. Hollis didn't think about it. She ran into the circle of his embrace like she could hide there from everything happening.

Will held her for a second, then turned and placed her behind him to shield her with his body. She slid her one usable arm around his waist from behind and held on.

He laid his arm over hers, making her stand tight against him. "Whatever you've got going on," he told Frankie, "just do it. Leave the two of us out of it."

As he spoke, he reached back and tapped his back pocket.

Hollis saw the phone.

She slid it out and swiped to unlock. No fingerprint, no pattern, no code. Those only slowed a person down when their life was in danger.

On the screen, Tate's contact was cued up. Hollis started typing a text.

"Get whatever that is."

She'd barely registered the words before the phone was snatched out of her hand. Will capitalized on the distraction to shove at the friend who'd been in the room with him, and then he punched the guy to the floor. All that, without barely moving. Just a quick twist of his hips and shoulders before rotating them back. She thanked God for all his years of combat training.

"She's tryna call out."

Hollis pressed her lips together. Will was so big, she could barely peer over his shoulder at Frankie. "What do you expect? You've already killed two people, and we're probably next."

"Nah. Doesn't fit the narrative that you'd kill Mr. FBI here." Frankie shrugged one shoulder, holding the gun pointed at Will's chest. "Not when you're obviously in on all of this together."

Her stepfather suddenly looked unrecognizable to her. He sneered at Will, gun still trained on him, and continued to craft his own account of what went down, "He keeps the cops busy, off your tails, see." He flicked his wrist so that now his gun pointed at Hollis. "You kill Sharleen and try to take the stash, so you can make your getaway. Me? I'm injured, but somehow manage to escape your clutches." His satisfied smile sickened her.

She shook her head. "Who are you?"

The words escaped her lips before she could think it through. Will's hand on her arm flexed, a show of solidarity—*or* his attempt to tell her to shush. But, how could she? This man wasn't the stepdad she'd known for years. Someone she'd tried desperately to get close to, her only shot at a "parent." Or so she'd thought. He was no more a parent to her than Sharleen was. She could see that now.

"None of it was real, was it?"

Frankie huffed a breath out his nose and shook his head.

"Well excuse me for being fooled along with *the rest of the town*. You pulled one over on all of us, not just me. All this time, I've been doing your work. Feeling sorry for you because of your limited mobility. Now I just feel bad for people whose suffering you diminished by being nothing but a lying, cheating conman."

Will squeezed her arm again. "Hol."

Whether that was him saying her name, or not, she wasn't sure. All she could think about was the blinding, hot fury raging through her. She wanted to throw something. Or punch a smug, deceitful, barely-limping man in the face. Except that he'd probably shoot her.

"Just do what you're gonna do. Get on with it!"

Will shifted in front of her, and only then did she realize she'd been screaming. Hollis lowered her chin and leaned her forehead to rest on the back of his shoulder. She wanted to collapse on the floor, sinking fast like her energy level. But then how would she fight back?

She should let go of Will. Allow him the space to fight if he decided he needed to. Had he brought a gun? She ran her hand from his waist and around to the back of his jacket, bracing herself back onto her heels in order to regain her balance without leaning all her weight on him.

She encountered the bulge at the back of his waistband.

Hollis stilled. Will's other hand came back and wrapped around her, tugging her against him. A clear signal to stay where she was and not do anything.

Hollis fought his hold for a second. Until she realized he was a federal agent and she was a glorified waitress. Not that waitresses couldn't protect themselves, but she probably wasn't one of them and would probably wind up getting Will killed. The same way she'd gotten that trucker shot.

"Tie them both up," Frankie said. "And search him for weapons."

She whimpered. Then realized the instruction given. She slipped her hand under the back of Will's jacket, pulled the gun out as carefully and discreetly as she could, and reached back to tuck it in the same spot on the waistband. Except, this time on *her*.

The other guy, who'd been here with Will when Frankie

shoved her in the kitchen, pulled plastic ties from a drawer and came over.

"Hands."

"I don't think I want to know why you have those here." She glanced at Frankie. There was no justification for the things he'd done, and she probably didn't know the half of it.

"Arrangements I've made with business associates are none of your business."

Hollis pressed her lips together. The guy tied up Will, and then shoved his face up against the wall as he patted Will down.

"Well, well, well. What do we have here?" The guy pulled up Will's pant leg to reveal a gun. He pulled it out and pocketed it.

The confiscated phone buzzed across the counter.

Frankie stared at it until it vibrated enough to teeter and fall over the edge and onto the floor. It shattered. "Oops." A second later he said, "Get them both out here in the hall."

"Closet?"

"Yep."

The two men seemed to understand the significance of that. Hollis had her hands tied together. She tried to face her wrists to each other, but the man snorted, and then stacked her hands.

"Unless you'd rather be shot?"

She held them still, and he circled them with the plastic. It bit into her skin as he tightened it further. "Ow."

He laughed.

"Hallway." Frankie motioned with the gun and backed out of the room.

Will rushed the man who'd tied him up. He slammed him against the counter, whipped around, and snatched up the second gun.

Frankie fired from the hallway. Will spun around, just in time, and stumbled away as the other man's breath caught in surprise. He slid to the floor, leaving a wet, red stain on the wall behind where he'd been standing.

"Hallway. Now."

Will went first, taking her hand so she stayed close. Their bound hands together. Shoved down the hall as one, where Frankie had a door open. "Both of you, inside."

Will stepped in first. Meeting the threat. Hollis followed. Just as she moved into the dark room, Frankie kicked the back of her knee.

She went down, landing with what sounded like a pop and she cried out. Frankie kicked her again—in the middle of her back this time—and pulled the gun from the back of her waistband. She spun on the floor, and he slammed the door in her face.

A second later, the lock was thrown. They were trapped in here.

Hollis didn't get up.

"Hey." Will crowded her.

She didn't care, just let the tears flow. Will grunted and sat down. His knees were almost in her face. How small was this "closet"? He tugged her onto his lap. She didn't want to squish him, but he didn't react to her weight on him, either.

Will lowered his arms over her head and rubbed up and down her back.

Hollis whimpered. "I wanted to do *something*."

Will just grunted again.

"I was trying to help." Now her knee felt like it was on fire, and she had one broken arm. She'd look like a freak with only one arm and one leg that worked. At least she was honest. Unlike Frankie.

"I know." Will just kept holding her, even though her hands were bound. "I'll figure out a way to get us out of this."

Upstairs, a woman screamed. Then another.

Hollis shuddered. "I was only trying to do the right thing." Instead she got strung along, she'd seen people murdered, and now she and Will were locked in a tiny, pitch-black closet.

A gun went off, and she flinched. One of the women screamed.

Crack.

The scream cut off.

Tears rolled down her face. Will said, "I can kick the door open. But I want Frankie and his gun out of here first."

"Those women…"

"Apparently, Athens is one of Frankie's business partners, because the girls were his."

She squeezed her eyes shut, even though it was just as dark as with them open. "My uncle." She could hardly believe any of this. "The diner." She moaned. So much death and destruction, it was hard to bear it all.

God. She didn't know what to say. Wasn't He supposed to take pain and give peace instead? Joy, and life. She needed all of those things right now when things were at their worst.

Frankie's unsteady gait pattered down the stairs above them. Will stiffened. She could hear her stepfather moving around.

"I can't believe I actually cared about him." She didn't really expect a response from Will. Not when there was nothing he could say that would make her feel better. "That I believed he cared about me. I just thought he was bad at showing it. I did everything I could to help him."

"I know." He shifted his face so his cheek was beside hers. "You didn't know, and no one will blame you. Not when he lied to *everyone.*"

Hollis had tried her whole life to earn love. It hadn't exactly panned out, but Will cared, even though she'd really done nothing for him. Evidently—she knew this because he'd told her a few weeks before—there was something in her that appealed to him, inside and out. Just like there was a whole lot of him that appealed to her. And she had to believe she was both lovable and worthy, whether she did the right thing all the time or not. Whether she was actually "worthy," or not. This had to be true in every area of her life.

Or it wasn't true at all.

She was either "enough" or she wasn't. And if she wasn't ready to accept that, then she wasn't ready to accept his love.

Sharleen hadn't seen the way she had strived to earn love. Frankie had ignored it. Neither cared. Only her friends seemed to be concerned about her.

Then there was Will. He'd lied, but the job he did was so important. After all, without him, she'd never have discovered the truth. Frankie would still be terrorizing people, and no one would be the wiser.

Above the rancid odor of the closet, a musty tang hit her nostrils. Thick air and a rough smell.

Will said, "Fire."

"What?" Hollis tried to move back. Will's arms were around her, so he had to lift them up and over her head to give her the space to lean away as far as she wanted to.

"Let me help you up."

She leaned on the wall while he turned, close enough she felt the brush of his clothing. "Will."

"If he's burning down the house, we can't wait. I'll kick the door down and either go for the gun, or if he's gone, we'll head for the closest door."

Fear raced through her. Despite being trapped, there was safety being in the closet, away from the immediate threat. Unless, of course, the house burned down around them.

"Ready?"

She grasped for him and found his arm. Hollis turned him to her and moved her bound hands up, feeling for his chin. She grasped it in her fingers and leaned in to press her lips against his. It didn't last long. It couldn't. They had to get out of here. "Will."

He followed her as she leaned away from him. His kiss lasting longer than hers, as though he never wanted to be anywhere else. Desperation. Apology. Passion. All of it was there as they said what they needed to say, without any words, what hadn't yet been spoken between them.

And then he pulled away. "Get as far back as you can."

He turned and kicked the closet door open.

A wall of flames roared on the other side.

26

A breeze ruffled his hair and collar. Will realized the front door had opened. He sucked in the biggest breath he could without coughing and yelled into the fire, "We need help!"

"Will?"

"Tate!" The private investigator. Of course, he'd known they were in the house. And, he now knew it was on fire. Will prayed he'd called for emergency services. *Thank You.* They'd survived so far. A fire wasn't going to be the thing that brought them down just yet.

Hollis grasped the back of his jacket, probably feeling the same relief he did. "We need to—" She coughed. "—out of here."

"I know." He looked back and saw a collection of coats hung on a rail. So, in addition to a heavily padlocked prison, this was also an actual closet they'd been shoved into.

Will wanted to yell for Tate to make sure Frankie didn't get away, but the priority here was getting him and Hollis out of here. And they were both injured. He pulled down two coats and used one to smother the flames that licked the other side of the closet door.

"Come on." He motioned for her to move with him, holding

her up with an arm around her waist. She was so strong, even while in obvious and serious pain from her arm and knee. The woman should probably be in a hospital. And that was exactly where they were going.

He had her lean against the wall, the glow of the flames reflected upon her face. But right now, that beautiful sight wouldn't be fully appreciated. With a campfire, he might be able to relax and watch the play of orange light her features. Not right now, though.

Will got more coats, and they did their best to smother the flames that roared across the floor and licked at the walls. It wasn't foolproof. His hands felt singed, his face far too hot. Like a really bad sunburn. Still, they got far enough that Will could logistically and safely hand Hollis over to Tate.

But he didn't.

Will had absolutely no intention of letting go of her. Ever.

"Come on." Tate held Hollis's other arm, and they all moved outside, off the front step and down the walk to the curb.

Will turned to Hollis. "Do you need to sit?"

When she nodded, lines of pain formed around her mouth, and so he had her lean against the hood of his car so she could take the weight off her knee.

Tate cut them both loose, and then his gaze shifted to the house. "Fire, police, and an ambulance are all on their way. But if Dean shows up first, I wouldn't be surprised."

Will touched Hollis's shoulders, aware his hands were shaking. He'd gotten her back, and while he'd wanted to get her back in one piece, she was more like a piece that was seriously battered. "You good?"

She grasped his elbow with her good hand and looked up at him, chewing on her lip while her eyes filled with tears. Will stepped close and pulled her into his arms. "I probably smell like smoke."

She chuckled. "Me too."

"I didn't notice."

That turned her chuckle into audible laughter. "You're such a liar." She shifted and he moved back, giving her a moment to say, "Thanks for being in that closet with me, and for coming to get me."

Will touched her forehead with his.

"Hate to break this up, but you both need to be looked at."

He turned to Tate.

The private investigator laughed at the expression on Will's face. "Dean is here."

Will sat on the hood beside Hollis, while the former SEAL checked her over. "How's construction going?"

"Got planning approval yesterday. Green lights all the way."

"Let me know if you need any help."

The SEAL flipped open a pocket knife and glanced at Will. "Yeah?"

"I did a lot of construction in high school and college."

"Sweet."

"What are you doing with that knife?"

Dean said, "Looking at your knee." Despite Will asking the question, Dean answered as though Hollis had. "But I have to cut your pants to see. Okay?"

She nodded. Will put his arm around her and tried inconspicuously to cough the scratch out of his throat. It didn't work.

"You both need to be admitted to the hospital."

Maybe. Will said, "When I know Frankie is in custody."

Tate said, "That's who had gone in with Hollis?"

Will nodded. "Did you see him come out?"

"I figured he was still in there." Tate waved at the house. "That the fire department would be pulling him out anytime now."

Sure enough, the truck was here, and they were headed into the house already.

Hollis said, "Frankie *is* West. He's the one behind all of this." Her voice was almost desperate as she tried to talk through the pain and smoke inhalation.

When she said no more, Will gave her a squeeze. He asked Tate, "Did you see anyone come out?"

"One guy, moving fast and carrying a duffel. But it wasn't you, so I came in to see if there was a way to get everyone out." Tate shook his head. "I couldn't get past the front door. If you guys hadn't gotten yourselves out, you'd still be in there."

Hollis said, "That had to have been Frankie leaving."

Tate frowned. "Moving that fast? He's not that able bodied."

As he spoke, Eric pulled up in his rental car followed by a line of police vehicles. The crowd of cops took barely a minute to circle them.

Will was the first to speak. "Frankie was behind it all. He's in the wind with, presumably, the resources to disappear."

Conroy said, "We'll find him."

Hollis said, "He's the one you've been looking for all this time, and he's been under your noses, fooling all of you. Fooling me." Her body was stiff, her voice angrier than he'd ever heard it. "He was the man running from the house," she told Tate, "you should have caught him."

"I shouldn't have tried to save you?"

"He killed four people today." Will let that sink in. "Three are in that house. A man, and also two women who were being held upstairs, apparently 'belonging' to Athens."

Conroy's lips thinned. He walked off toward the fire chief.

Will told Eric, "Frankie needs to be found and brought to justice."

He had been protecting Hollis, making sure they got out of that situation alive. The idea it had cost him his arrest wasn't an entirely comfortable notion, even though he knew he'd done the right thing. Just as Tate had done, trying to help them. Even if Hollis might not agree.

But that didn't mean Frankie could be left alone to make a run for it and disappear, never to be found again. The man needed to be in cuffs. It was past time. Someone needed to answer for the years of crime that had been rampant in this community.

Eric studied him.

Will said, "I watched him kill a man. Then he locked me and Hollis in a closet. The two women who were upstairs? We heard them scream, and then there were gunshots. He left us to die in that fire."

Eric nodded. "Copy that."

Will didn't have to tell him that he'd write up a full report. That he would more than happily testify in court as part of the case. When it went to trial. This was Will's investigation, and he would see it through to the end.

While he also took care of Hollis.

There was a lot to discuss, and even more to figure out. Will wasn't entirely sure what his future held. What he did know was that in three weeks, he would not be taking another undercover assignment in a new town. No contacting Hollis for the duration?

No way. That wasn't happening.

Eric read it all on his face. Will knew that when his colleague nodded. "I'll make some calls."

Dean pressed his fingers on Hollis's knee, and she hissed out a breath.

Will shot the man a scathing look.

"It's sprained, badly. They'll probably x-ray it anyway, but I don't think anything is broken." Dean straightened to his full height. "Probably doesn't feel too good, right?" He pulled off his protective gloves. "Ambulance is here."

Will helped Hollis stand, and they made their way slowly to the back of the ambulance.

"You wanna take your own car, or ride with me?"

Will handed her over to the EMTs and turned to Eric. "What?"

"To go after Frankie."

"I'm not going after Frankie. You are."

Eric's eyebrows lifted.

"I'm going to the hospital with Hollis."

"Are you injured?"

Will said, "I need to be checked out, but I'm going to stick with Hollis. Just in case Frankie shows up there with hostile intent." That wasn't the reason he would stay with her. But it would feel good to be close to her. "I'm not leaving her."

"Huh."

"Text me when you locate him. I'd like to be part of the takedown, if I can be, but I'm not going on another wild goose chase. Not if it leaves Hollis in danger."

"This is your investigation."

Will nodded. "True. Doesn't mean I have to be the arresting officer, though. Conroy probably wouldn't mind that honor. I'd like to see it happen. But I've done what I came here to do."

And wasn't that the truth? His job had been to find the source. West had been identified, and Conroy would be motivated to bring Frankie in now. Along with all of his officers. That meant it wasn't Will's job alone.

After working solo for as long as he had, it was strange to leave it to others. But Will knew down to his soul that it was the right thing to do.

And it felt like being set free.

He didn't have to take it all on by himself. These people were his team, law enforcement colleagues who were more than capable of finding and arresting Frankie.

"That's it?" Eric said, "I just call you when it's done, and you walk off into the sunset."

"I'll be at the hospital."

"I should go then. Seems like I have work to do." Eric turned and strode back to Tate, his brother-in-law.

Will figured the FBI agent had plenty of motivation to bring down Frankie. Especially considering this was a town where his extended family lived. Will was the new guy, having been here not that long. Still, it was beginning to feel like home. Last

Chance was a place he'd finally found something worth sticking around for.

As he climbed into the ambulance and smiled at the shocked look on Hollis's face, he wondered what she would think about staying here. She'd been about to leave. That was about Sharleen and Frankie. Her mom had been killed, right in front of her. Frankie would be arrested.

Did Hollis want to talk about staying here? Will would consider anywhere, if that was where she would be.

It suddenly occurred to him that the case, for him, was basically over. He only awaited word that Frankie was in cuffs.

He needed to call his dad. Let the old man know he was all right this time, like all the other times. Hollis might have lost her whole family, but could Will give her a new—a better—one? People who genuinely cared about her.

The idea lit a fire of hope in him.

"I need help!" A firefighter lumbered over, carrying a young woman in his arms. "She's still alive."

Hollis gasped. Will said, "What about the other one?"

The firefighter shook his head and handed the woman to the EMT. She was loaded on the other stretcher. Blood coated her front. A lot of blood.

The EMT glanced at Will. "Get the doors shut." Then he called to his partner in the front seat, "Let's go!"

The ambulance pulled out a second after Will had the doors shut. He sat beside Hollis, and they watched the medic work on the young woman while they raced to the hospital.

They took the girl in first.

Then Hollis was checked in.

A nurse tried to get him to get checked in as well, but Will shook his head. "In a minute. I need to make a call first."

She didn't look impressed. Will ignored her expression and pulled out his cell phone. He dialed. Two rings, and the call was answered.

"Hey…Pop. It's Will."

27

Hollis was immediately aware she wasn't alone. "Will..." But—it wasn't him. Though the line of the man's shoulders was different, there was a comforting familiarity there.

"I'm Carlyle Briar. Will's dad." He sat forward in the chair beside her hospital bed.

Hollis tried to move. One leg didn't feel right. Frantically she felt down over the blanket. It was huge, her knee wrapped in some kind of bandage.

"They said it's a bad sprain, but they also said to tell you, 'Dean was right again.'" He shook his head. "Whatever that means." He paused. "You okay, Hollis?"

"Where's Will?"

After that speech about staying with her while the rest of the cops brought in her stepdad, she'd figured he would be here when she woke up. Unless he'd changed his mind?

And what time was it, anyway? Right now she didn't know what day it was, either.

"Uh...Carlyle. It's nice to meet you."

His lips curled into a smile. "Don't ask what my mother was thinking when she named me, because I have no idea. Most people call me Briar, since most people I know are military." He shifted, and she saw tattoos up both forearms and on his biceps, below the sleeves of his T-shirt. "We'll have to figure out what you're gonna call me."

Probably she would call him by his name, right?

"Will calls me Pop, but you could use dad all the same. Wouldn't matter to me."

Hollis pressed her lips together. She didn't want to ask again where Will was, but she really wanted to know. And not just because she suddenly had the urge to ask him what on earth his dad was talking about right now. There was so much unsaid.

But Will wasn't here.

"Oh, and to answer your question." Carlyle touched the side of his head. "Nearly forgot. You've been asleep about fourteen hours now. Long enough for me to get here from Texas. Long enough for Eric to find Frankie. Will went to see that he was brought in without incident. He said he'd be gone less than an hour."

"Oh. Okay."

"It's not ideal, I know." Will's dad said, "He was hoping you'd wait to wake up until he got back." He grinned. "Just my luck, I get to see the pretty green of your eyes before he's able to come bumbling back in, saying the wrong thing, and scare you off. Unless, of course, I do it first."

Hollis smiled.

"There we go."

He was trying to put her at ease. She was grateful for that. Carlyle stood. "How's the pain? The nurse said to get her if you woke up in too much discomfort."

"It's...manageable."

"I'm thinking you've been through enough." He nodded. "The woman my son is in love with can have better than 'manageable.' So, I'll be talking to the nurse." Carlyle leaned a hip against the side of her hospital bed. "Now I guess I know why I woke up in the middle of the night last couple of nights. Got that urge to pray, like my mom always told me she did in my wild younger days. Now I'm praying for my son. And you, though I didn't know it at the time."

Hollis just stared at him, unsure what to say.

"I've been praying nonstop, like I do whenever Will is undercover." He smiled, almost looking embarrassed, and patted her hand. "I know you don't know me, but I'm glad you're all right. And I'm sorry about your family."

"Thanks."

"Will is going to be back soon. You just rest. Anything you need, let me know."

He wandered to the door and stepped out, giving her another pleasant smile before shutting the door.

Frankie was actually being brought in. She let that sink in.

She thought of the girl who'd been carried down from upstairs, and she wondered if she made it. And what life would be like for her, having lived through that? Her mind took in the scream of the girl who got shot. The one who didn't make it.

She heard the gunshot blast and it all played out in her mind again, but this time, it was her mom's blood spray that she saw. The slump of her body. Hollis choked back a sob.

"Hey."

She sucked in a breath. It wasn't Carlyle this time. Will shut the door and came over. He sat on the edge of the bed and leaned close to tuck hair behind her ear, while she struggled to control the tears that threatened to spill.

"Everything is okay now."

She sniffed. Nodded.

"Frankie is in jail. Conroy got him, and they're taking him to county lockup now. He's not going anywhere. Athens has also been brought in, along with a half-dozen guys associated with one or both of them."

Hollis pressed her lips together.

"There's nothing to be afraid of."

That might be true, but Hollis still pulled him to her and buried her face in his neck, while he wrapped his arms around her. She held on with her good hand, and also with the fingers sticking out of the fresh bandage on her other one.

They sat in that embrace for a while. She heard the door open and then quickly close again.

This was what she wanted. But Hollis couldn't help feeling those old insecurities flare up, threatening to steal the happiness she'd found. Trying to make her believe she didn't deserve good things.

"My dad said you were in some pain."

"I'm okay." She gave him a squeeze with her good hand and then lay back. "Thank you."

His expression softened. "For what?"

"How about…everything?"

"I love you."

Hollis was so surprised by the abrupt change of direction in the conversation that she laughed aloud.

"Oh no. Why would that be funny? Is it too soon?"

She tried to smile, even though she was still kind of crying. "It's not too soon."

Will swiped tears from her cheeks with his thumbs.

"It's only funny because I feel the same way, but I didn't know how I was going to tell you."

"Just tell me," he said. "Say it straight."

After being lied to and manipulated her whole life, she figured that was a good idea. And a welcome change. "I love you, Will Briar. Or Phil Tilley." She ran her thumb over the tattoo on his neck. "Whoever you are, or whoever you have to pretend to be for work."

"This is going to fade in about six weeks."

Hollis shrugged. "It kind of suits you."

"You suit me. The tattoo, I don't really care. So long as you're in this with me."

"In…what exactly?"

"Life. All of it. A relationship, and the chance to see where this is going. Work. Church. Eventually, family."

"You want all that?" She figured she was up for it, if he was there too.

He nodded. "What do you say?"

This sounded oddly like a proposal to her. Though it was much too soon for that. Or was it? Hollis figured she knew enough to know that she didn't want to end up with anyone else. Only Will knew the battle she'd faced, because he was right there beside her the whole time. Fighting for her. Saving her, the way she'd saved him from that fire.

Thank You, Lord.

"I do want to go to church."

"Okay." He was waiting for more.

Before she could say anything, the door opened. "Did she say yes yet?" That was Carlyle.

Will groaned. "Not yet, Pop. Can you be patient?"

"No, son. This old dog isn't gonna learn that particular trick."

Sounded like he didn't even want to try. And from the look on his face, Hollis figured he thought that was more amusing than anything else.

The nurse came in as well, and Hollis was distracted answering questions and taking more medicine. She wanted to ask when she would be released, but walking didn't sound particularly pleasant right now, so she figured she was okay to stay put just a little longer.

In the corner of the room, Will and his dad had a hushed conversation. She could see the closeness between them in the way they faced each other. The light in their eyes, and the crinkle of humor around his father's.

The nurse left, and Carlyle gave Will a shove toward her. "Go get 'er."

"Nice, Pop. Real classy."

The old man winked at her and then left.

Will dug in his pocket, then sat beside her in the same spot as before. "Continuing our theme of it not being too soon…"

He held up what was in his hand. "If you don't want it right now, I understand. But I'd like to give it to you eventually. Pop brought it with him."

She frowned.

"It's the ring he gave my mother."

Hollis sucked in a breath. "I love you."

"I love you, too. I hope, at least one day, you'll wear it."

EPILOGUE

"To have and to hold." The preacher waited while the groom recited the words. "For richer, for poorer." He waited again.

Halfway back in the church pews, Hollis turned to Will who was sat beside her wearing a suit. She had a dress and heels on, her hair down and wavy around her shoulders. He'd said that was his favorite. And not the only reason she'd decided to never wear her hair in a bun the rest of her life.

He must have sensed her attention because he turned to her.

"I love you."

Will smiled.

Up on the stage, the pastor had the bride recite the same vows to her soon-to-be husband.

"I know." Will touched his lips to hers.

She didn't turn back to the front. "I'd like that ring now."

It had been an unspoken agreement. He'd wait, but as soon as she was ready she could ask him for his mother's ring.

Over the past few weeks, Carlyle had stuck around. The two of them had arranged for her to buy the diner, and they'd been fixing it up for her. Which had turned into Will joining the crew completing construction on Dean's therapy center.

He'd bought a house on the lake.

His dad had bought twelve acres on the edge of town and moved here as well.

They were three days away from the grand opening of the new diner, which she was now the proud owner of. Life didn't look too different on the surface. But in all the ways that counted, she was new, and her entire existence was different. So different.

Thank You, Lord.

New relationships. A new job. Hope. A future.

The pastor said, "I now pronounce you husband and wife."

Ignoring the ceremony, Will dipped his hand into the inside pocket of his suit jacket. He'd been carrying the ring with him this whole time. Waiting for her.

"I love you."

Will slid the ring onto her left hand and touched his lips to hers. Looking more relieved than she was comfortable with. He'd really been worried? Hollis determined then not to make him wait for the next step.

"Soon."

He nodded. "Good."

Up on the stage, the pastor said, "It's with great honor I present to you, Mr. and Mrs. Conroy Barnes."

Hollis grinned at Will, and then clapped with everyone else to celebrate Mia and Conroy.

Hope.

A future.

Hollis watched the smile on Mia's face, knowing exactly how she felt.

I hope you enjoyed *Expired Plot*, please consider leaving a review, it really helps others find their next read! Turn the page for the

first 2 chapters of the 7th story in the Last Chance County
series: *Expired Getaway*

U.S.A. TODAY BESTSELLING AUTHOR
LISA PHILLIPS PRESENTS

EXPIRED GETAWAY

LAST CHANCE COUNTY BOOK SEVEN

Copyright 2020 Lisa Phillips

All rights reserved. This book or any portion thereof may not be reproduced or used in any manner whatsoever without the express written permission of the publisher except for the use of brief quotations in a book review.

eBook ISBN: 979-8-88552-055-3

Paperback ISBN: 979-8-88552-056-0

Publisher: Two Dogs Publishing, LLC. Idaho, USA.

Cover design: Ryan Schwarz

Edited by: Jen Weiber

1

Denver, Colorado.

The back door to the accountant's office had been broken and busted into. The keypad smashed up, obliterated by the butt of someone's gun. Or so she assumed.

Bridget had a phone, but 911 was the last thing on her mind.

All she could think of as she drew out her gun and deposited her pack by the back wall was wondering who had been on shift tonight. She'd been out of town for two days delivering a care package to one of their clients. It was a regular enough occurrence, but traveling to Caracas to do so wasn't. Being discovered there by cartel guys while fishing the client out of a dicey situation and running for their lives? Also not so much.

Bridget had very nearly been shot right before stashing the client somewhere safe. Afterward, she flew to Mexico City and met with a doctor, passed out for two days from exhaustion, and managed to miss her meeting time.

Now that she was finally here, she discovered the office had been broken into.

Bridget didn't believe in coincidences. But of all the enemies the accountant's office had, she didn't have the first idea who might be inside.

Or what they wanted.

Bridget cast a longing glance at her backpack. She didn't like leaving it unattended, but it could hinder her if she had to fight.

She eased the door open with her foot and stepped into the back hallway.

A muffled grunt echoed from the main office.

The place wasn't big. A strip mall storefront with a small unused apartment above—a safe house when one was needed. Bridget made up one quarter of the four employees. The boss was currently out of town on vacation with her husband. That left Clarke and Sasha. If someone had broken in while Sasha was working late, they'd be dead already.

That left Clarke.

Her sometimes-on-again/sometimes-off-again boyfriend had made it clear before she left that he wanted things to go to the "next level." Bridget didn't even know what that meant. Or why she was dragging her feet over him.

She needed to tide him over with some sort of excuse until she figured out for herself what her deal was with him.

Bridget crept down the hall to the door at the end, ajar. Beyond, the main office was lit. They'd painted the front windows so no one could see inside.

Another cry sounded, not so muffled now.

Bridget whispered, "Clarke."

She should get in there and save him from whatever was happening. Still, part of her wanted to wait so she had a better idea of what she was getting into. Another part of her—one she wasn't sure she liked—wanted to see what he'd do. How he might handle this. As though his mettle hadn't been tested already in this job, and she needed to put him through the wringer all over again. She didn't need to see the depth of his skills. That was selfish.

"You will tell us what we want to know." The accented voice

held the strain of authority. Someone not used to being ignored, who was accustomed to making someone pay dearly for such lack of judgment.

A shudder began but Bridget locked it down like she always did. She needed steady hands and a calm mind. Something she'd worked on for years, battling her fear to the place she could be strong. Valued.

Not the beat-up, broken-down teen who'd left Last Chance in the middle of the night without ever looking back. The lingering trauma flared on occasion—like when she saw blood. Given the last few days, her history was pretty close to the surface.

But she couldn't let it penetrate. That would only leave her useless.

Bridget kicked the door open. She clocked the two guys in suits right away. Clarke stood behind his desk across from them. Unsure. Debating. He started to speak.

The door behind her hit the wall with a thud. Both suited guys shifted to her. Before they could face the new threat, Clarke pulled a gun from his desk and shot twice.

Both men fell to the ground.

Bridget blinked, but the prominent feeling that settled upon her was relief. It might seem harsh, but in their business, hesitation meant death. And given the last two days, she wasn't willing to take any chances. After the mission she'd just been on, Bridget knew something wasn't right.

She glanced around. "Are there more of them?"

Clarke stumbled back and sat heavily on the desktop before sliding sideways and falling to the cheap carpet. Blood trickled down the side of his face from a nasty gash on his temple. "Bridget. Hey."

"What is going on?" She strode over and held out her free hand. He'd killed those two men. "You good?"

Clarke clasped her wrist way too tight and nearly pulled her over as he stood. Once at his full height, he barely matched hers despite the fact she was wearing sneakers and not heels. She had at least two inches on him. Clarke flung his arms around her and squeezed, her arms—and the gun—smashed between them.

"Oof." Pain sliced through her middle—a bruised rib from yesterday. "Let go, Clarke."

He didn't. "I'm so glad you're here. I knew I'd have to take them out, but the element of surprise…" He squeezed once more and leaned back. "Works every time."

Bridget extricated herself from his arms. "So it was just the two of them?"

She moved to the closest one and took a look. Could be Capeira's goons, but she'd left Caracas two days ago. Had they really caught up to her this fast? There was no way they could've found the accountant's office that quickly.

"You see them," Clarke said. "There are two."

As though she couldn't do simple math, or needed what she'd seen with her own eyes explained to her. Bridget might not have been a particularly stellar student in high school, but she had skills. And a brain.

She tried to figure out what was up with him. "What did they say to you?"

"They wanted access to the computer systems. Of course, I would die before I ever gave them that."

The back door had been busted in to grant these men entry. He'd probably been taken by surprise. Hit over the head and disoriented before they demanded what they wanted. No one who worked here would ever give armed intruders anything. Except for a bullet.

She was just glad it had been Clarke and not her. She knew how to use her weapon, but only did so when it was a matter of life or death. Sneaking up on two men whose intentions she didn't know? That wasn't honorable.

Plus…she'd already killed someone this week.

Bridget walked to the second man he'd shot. A gun lay close

to his hand, fallen from his fingertips. He had a scar just below the base of his thumb. It had been carved there. "These guys are both underlings."

She straightened in time to catch Clarke eyeing the discarded weapon. "There should be a driver or a lieutenant with them."

No way would someone who knew what this place was actually trust a mission like this to two guys who hung on the bottom rungs of the ladder.

Bridget started to turn. Clarke was far too close to her.

He touched her shoulders, but the weight of his arms proved too heavy for it to be considered sweet or comfortable. "I'm so glad you're here." He shifted his body closer, but it wasn't comforting.

It was a threat.

"You probably saved my life." He let out a depreciating laugh. "If I was willing to admit it."

"You just did, but all I did was distract them." She tried to step back, but he didn't let go.

Clarke's gaze shifted over her shoulder. Holding her still.

Someone else was here.

Bridget held back the reaction that wanted out. She still had her gun. She could shoot Clarke right now. Instead, she brought her knee up between his. High enough to make contact, but still like she hadn't noticed it wasn't just the two of them here.

He doubled over.

"Clarke, you let a woman go when it's clear she wants to be free." It was a good point to make, but it became really clear really fast that it wasn't *the* point she should have focused on when a fist smashed into her cheekbone as soon as she spun around. A flash of pain doubled her over. Bridget blinked and stumbled back from yet another suited man.

Ouch.

He pried the gun from her fingers. She tried to grasp it, but by that time Clarke had recovered. He twisted her fingers almost to breaking point. She cried out. With her free hand, Bridget punched him in the stomach as hard as she could.

"Quit messing around and get her secured." Another heavily-accented voice.

Clarke pulled her hands behind her back. "I told you she would come here."

"Mmm."

Bridget struggled, fighting against the man until she found herself staring down the barrel of a Glock, pointed right at her. Beyond it stood a man whose brother she had shot two days ago. She gritted her teeth. Was he here for revenge?

"Your brother nearly shot me." He'd also compromised their client, but Bridget wasn't going to bring her into this. The woman needed a new identity and somewhere to go—both of which Bridget was supposed to figure out tonight. Until then, the client had to lay low. The Capeiras weren't going to find her.

She turned to Clarke. "You're the one who sold her out and told Benito Capeira where she was. Aren't you?"

His expression hardened. "They made me do it. They said they'd kill my mother if I didn't."

Bridget's overblown sense of empathy for the underdog flared to life inside her. At the same time, she tried to figure out if he was even telling the truth.

Capeira laughed. Smaller than his brother, Enrico was still built like a powerhouse. She needed to not underestimate him the way she had with Benito. That only landed her with a broken rib before she was forced to shoot him. Both men's reputations spoke of a ruthless need to be obeyed at all times.

Those who did not? Their bodies were never found.

Until the client discovered their secrets and took that information to the Justice Department. Instead of being given the case, she'd been told to go find "actual evidence." Bridget had heard enough. She was going to help.

She'd also thought Clarke would help.

Guess not.

"A chair, I think." Enrico stepped back and motioned with his gun. "Make it look like she fell asleep exhausted and smoking a cigarette. Accidents happen."

Clarke shoved her into a chair. "I thought we were doing a gas leak."

"Like I said, 'accidents.'"

Bridget looked up at her colleague. Before she could say anything, he ran the back of his hand down her cheek. "I'll be heartbroken. But I'll find someone else."

Before she took her next break, he raised his hand and pistol whipped her with her gun. Everything went black.

The next thing Bridget knew was that she couldn't breathe. She tried to move. Her face was smashed against the carpet. Using both hands, she did a push up and got her knees under her. No restraints. They had to have left her free to make the "accident" look real.

When she lifted up, the temperature of the room registered within her.

Then the smell.

Bridget launched herself toward the back hall. She stumbled, slammed her shoulder against the corner of the wall, and cried out. She didn't have time for more injuries. The building was about to explode.

She braced the wall with one hand and raced the other direction, down the hall to the back door she'd come in.

An explosion ripped through the building. The force blew apart the door and flipped her over. She slammed onto the asphalt outside and rolled. A moan escaped her lips, but she needed to see it. She needed to know it was still there.

Her backpack.

Bridget crawled to the wall beside the spot the door had been just a moment ago. She shifted rubble and tugged over her pack to hold it close as she dug inside for her phone. Relief washed over her, though this wasn't done.

Far from it.

She pulled up her texts and sent one to her boss.

CODE RED.

Nothing needed to be—or could be—salvaged from the building. It was all saved to an encrypted server. They would move on. Rebuild. Once Bridget took care of the threat, and Clarke.

She forced her legs to take her weight and start walking. The last thing she needed was to still be here when the cops arrived.

A second later she got a reply with an address.

GET HERE ASAP.

Bridget sagged against the siding of a neighboring building. Go there? After all these years, that was the last place she wanted to be. But orders were orders. She had to head home.

To Last Chance.

2

Last Chance

"I was hoping you'd be here." The woman who'd sidled up to him lifted a beer bottle and took a sip.

Aiden Donaldson, Last Chance police officer—currently off duty—tried to remember what her name was, but for the life of him, he couldn't. He smiled. "It's good to see you." Then turned back to the group of kids bowling.

His kid was up, so he squeezed through the crowd of moms and children—including the birthday girl—and made his way to where Sydney waited for a ball to come out.

"This purple one will work."

"I'm waiting for the pink one."

Behind them, a group of first grade girls erupted into laughter. The pink ball came out.

"Ready?"

"I want to do it by myself."

Aiden bit back what he wanted to say and squeezed down on his back teeth while he sent her a closed-mouth smile.

His little redhead missed nothing. "I can do it."

"And I'll be right here while you do." Aiden walked with her to the ramp that'd been dragged over. All she had to do was push the ball and watch it sail down the alley.

She hefted the ball onto the ramp that was little more than three bars of metal welded into a frame. The ball started to roll, so he put out his hand. It didn't need to go down before she had the chance to push it.

He lifted his gaze to the face of his six year old. "Ready, Beautiful?"

"Ms. Maggie said you'd like my dress." Her fingers lifted off the ball, and it started to roll toward his hand. "We got the blue one because it's your favorite color."

"That it is." Aiden grinned and saw the next kid waiting. "Ready?"

She nodded. He moved his hand and Sydney pushed the ball, her tongue stuck out from between her teeth in concentration. Aiden didn't watch the ball. He watched her face, garnering enough information from that as to what was happening down the alley.

Tomorrow he would be back on swing shift for the next four nights before he got two days off. That meant Sydney would be with the sitter after she got out of holiday kids club and in bed before he was home.

But he got breakfast, and they tried to live it up with the time they had. Aiden was a pancake artist using squirt bottles and food coloring. He could make a rainbow, and he was working on perfecting a unicorn, though it wasn't going well.

"I knocked down three!"

Aiden picked her up and spun her, even though she said she was too big for that. Sydney slapped his cheeks and blew a raspberry on his forehead.

He set her down, grinning.

"Cake!" Sydney ran off to her friends, and he wandered back to where he'd left his water cup. The mom with her beer watched him. The look on her face wasn't one he wanted to entertain.

Still, as he moved toward the table of kids all eating a slice of pizza before their cake, she also moved. When he reached the edge of the birthday party, she was beside him.

"You're a pretty good dad."

He glanced aside to see her eyeing him over her beer again. "And that's a surprise?"

The woman shrugged a slender shoulder. Too slender, by his estimation. "Single dad, right?"

"What does that have to do with it?"

"Usually dads aren't all that interested is all."

Aiden watched Sydney reach for her cup. He winced as she nearly knocked over another kid's soda.

"It's nice. That's what I'm saying."

He turned. "Which one is yours?"

"Oh. None." She motioned with her head toward the bar. "I just hang out here."

Aiden's stomach turned over.

"They're so cute at this age, aren't they? Then they turn into unholy terrors at the drop of a hat if they don't get what they want. Am I right?"

"Not in my experience."

He wanted to walk away. To stand closer to Sydney like a helicopter dad. Which he pretty much was, but only because he was the only person in the world there to watch her back. The sitter was amazing and he didn't know how he would do it without her and his army of church ladies to help, but at the end of the day, Aiden was alone in this.

"Huh." The woman blinked over her beer.

As a father and also a police officer, he needed to stick near this woman and try to get her to open up about her intentions here.

"It's more like, sometimes, she's not a kid at all. She's a tiny teenager." Aiden smiled, though the precise teenager Sydney reminded him of flashed in his mind.

There hadn't been much of a relationship between the two

of them, and they'd been barely out of high school. A summer romance gone wrong, if they could even say it had gone anywhere in the first place. Months later he'd found out she'd died in childbirth. That he was a father. Social services had asked him first if he wanted to raise the baby. As the father listed, he'd have had to give up his parental rights otherwise.

Give up the chance to pour love into a beautiful, innocent child of his own?

No way.

The woman barked out a rusty laugh. "Welp, I see my friends. I hate to love you and leave you, but I gotta go, gorgeous."

Aiden didn't even know what to say. He kept his mouth shut. He had no intention of setting her straight. There were no sparks between them. He was who he was—a twenty-four-year-old police officer and single dad to a six-year-old daughter.

Not most people's idea of a stellar beginning to adult life. No parties. An online degree. He knew more about assembling furniture and French braids than he knew about fraternities. But he wouldn't have it any other way.

Sydney had healed everything inside him that was broken. Aiden didn't want to know who he would be without her.

She tugged on his hand right then.

He looked down. "Pit stop?"

"Yes." She held his hand until they separated, and then she went into the ladies' room while Aiden waited outside. It still made him nervous to trust other people's goodness, but this was a small town and a lot of people knew their little family unit.

Aiden checked his emails while he waited, most of which were about the police post-holiday bash happening in a few days. No one was free to party during the holidays, so they did it mid-January.

The woman who'd tried to pick him up had chosen a new target, a guy at the bar. Worn jeans and steel toe boots. He wore a faded white sweater and had sunglasses on his head.

As he watched them, she pulled something from the back pocket of her jeans and exchanged it for what the man had. Plastic wrap, bundled up. The contents weren't something he could see, but experience and instinct indicated crack. Whether it was another illegal substance or that one, it didn't matter. It wasn't good.

The man squeezed her hip and she walked off, headed for a door that read, "Employees Only."

Aiden pulled up a text thread with his sergeant who was at work tonight and laid out what he'd just seen.

"Can we play at the arcade before we go?"

He looked down at Syd. "Probably not. It's pretty late, and we have church in the morning." After lunch, he would be on shift until past midnight.

"Donuts for breakfast?"

His phone buzzed. "Absolutely."

She jumped up and down. "Yes!"

Aiden read the text from Sergeant Basuto. An officer on duty was on the way. He eyed the door the woman had disappeared through while they made their way back to the party in time to sing and for Sydney to watch her friend open the doll they'd bought her.

He moved to Sydney and crouched to whisper. "Stay here with your friends. I'll be back in a few minutes, okay?" The birthday girl's mom seemed to have it all in hand, so he went to the Employees Only door and pulled out his badge. Just in case.

Aiden had a weapon on him but didn't get it out. All he needed to do was make sure the woman hadn't left. If she had, he wanted a description of her car. Or a plate number.

If she exited this way, he would talk to the manager about surveillance. Interview customers and staff, find out if the woman was a regular. Methodical actions that would get him in another conversation with that woman—one where he explained the seriousness of her actions. He'd make sure she knew help was available if she needed it, or caution her to get a lawyer if the situation warranted that.

He flashed his badge to the bartender who lifted his chin, then pushed through the door. The hall beyond was empty.

Three doors on both sides. One open. He moved to it, listening for…voices. At the door, he peered in.

"I said I did, didn't I?" Her tone wavered as a sliver of fear crept in.

The man she faced was taller, muscled. He wore slacks, black shoes, and a buttoned white shirt. Still, despite the professional clothing, there was an air of lethality about him.

Aiden cleared his throat.

The woman spun around while the man turned more slowly to find him there.

He decided to just pretend. "I'm totally lost. Is there a bathroom down this way?"

"Get him out of here." The man turned to his desk.

That left the woman to cross and jerk her head toward her shoulder. "Let's go. There's no bathroom over here. This is employees only."

"You work here?"

She led him to the door. "Just get out of here."

He held it open for her. She shook her head at his gentlemanly move and strode off. He spotted the person Basuto had sent and made his way to Officer Frees, at the same time watching where she went off to.

A group of men at the far end of the bar. The woman passed them. She said something low before heading for the front door, pushing it open to go outside.

"That her?" Frees eyed the woman's retreating form.

Aiden nodded.

"I got it. You get back to Syd."

Frees strode after her. He angled his radio to his mouth to speak as he headed out the front door. Aiden went back to the party, compiling his thoughts. Drug deal, and she was affiliated with the bowling alley. Whoever that guy was in the office, Aiden would talk to the sergeant about him. This could easily be a big case for the department. Though, given what they'd been through in recent months—this whole past year, basically—no one wanted to dip their toe into a huge problem so quickly.

Of course, they would if it became necessary. But a shark known as "West" had been swimming in the local pool for years. The result? Near devastation. Months of investigation down twists and blind corners. The cost to the department had been huge.

"Daddy." Syd slammed into him, and he lifted her again because she still let him do it. "Did you get that perp?"

Aiden grinned. "I'm not working. I'm hanging out with you." Never mind that no cop used the word "perp." Ever. "Is the party done?"

She eyed him. "I'm still hungry."

"So we should stop for broccoli on the way home?"

Syd made a mock-gagging noise. "Ice cream!"

Aiden blew a raspberry on her cheek. "As you wish."

He set her down, and they said their goodbyes to the birthday girl before turning to the front door of the bowling alley.

The guy from the office stood by the Employees Only door. Arms folded.

Watching him.

Continue reading *Expired Getaway* now - Find out where by visiting LastChanceCounty.com

OTHER BOOKS IN THE LAST CHANCE COUNTY SERIES

Book 1: Expired Refuge
Book 2: Expired Secrets
Book 3: Expired Cache
Book 4: Expired Hero
Book 5: Expired Game
Book 6: Expired Plot
Book 7: Expired Getaway
Book 8: Expired Betrayal
Book 9: Expired Flight
Book 10: Expired End

Also Available in 2 collections!
Books 1-5
Books 6-10

ABOUT THE AUTHOR

Follow Lisa on social media to find out about new releases and other exciting events!

Visit Lisa's Website to sign up for her mailing list to get FREE books and be the first to learn about new releases and other exciting updates!

https://www.authorlisaphillips.com

www.ingramcontent.com/pod-product-compliance
Lightning Source LLC
LaVergne TN
LVHW040737250326
834688LV00031B/332